T0354860

A World-Peace
Generating-Drug

A World-Peace
Generating-Drug

ZVEE GILEAD, PhD

A WORLD-PEACE GENERATING-DRUG

Copyright © 2024 Zvee Gilead, PhD.

All rights reserved. No part of this book may be used or reproduced by any means, graphic, electronic, or mechanical, including photocopying, recording, taping or by any information storage retrieval system without the written permission of the author except in the case of brief quotations embodied in critical articles and reviews.

iUniverse books may be ordered through booksellers or by contacting:

iUniverse
1663 Liberty Drive
Bloomington, IN 47403
www.iuniverse.com
844-349-9409

Because of the dynamic nature of the Internet, any web addresses or links contained in this book may have changed since publication and may no longer be valid. The views expressed in this work are solely those of the author and do not necessarily reflect the views of the publisher, and the publisher hereby disclaims any responsibility for them.

Any people depicted in stock imagery provided by Getty Images are models, and such images are being used for illustrative purposes only.
Certain stock imagery © Getty Images.

ISBN: 978-1-6632-6079-6 (sc)
ISBN: 978-1-6632-6078-9 (e)

Library of Congress Control Number: 2024904377

Print information available on the last page.

iUniverse rev. date: 03/26/2024

CONTENTS

INTRODUCTION

THE PRESENT NOVEL CONTAINS A **fictional story** that escribes the invention, production, and the clinical trials, of an anti-depressant drug called, FBS-SER. This drug exists only in the fertile imagination of the author, and has the capability to generate a total world-peace However, this fictional novel brings also real basic scientific information on the way new drugs are developed. It also describes the clinical trials necessary for certification of drugs by the FDA. Moreover .and not the least, the novel brings information on a variety of scientific subjects in a concise way. To compile all this informational "Reader's Digest issue", I gathered information from many sources and wrote them in a way which would save the reader much time trying to find and assimilate a lot of complicated scientific data. The scientific information that I brought is accurate, although somewhat simplified for the sake of clarity. It is also based on the author's personal knowledge.

Some scientific descriptions in the book may bore readers whose studies did not include biology, biochemistry, organic chemistry, and psychiatry. Also, it describes some psychiatric ailments that most people shy away from. However, all intelligent persons in our times would certainly benefit by reading about the scientific subjects and the psychiatric ailments.

The novel also contains a romantic love-story between the two main protagonists. In this love story, the female protagonist undergoes love pangs and turmoil until the male protagonist acquiesces.

You wish to jump into the novel and help the female partner. Later, you also wish to continue your participation in this love affair and carry it into your day.

CHAPTER 1

The assembly of the professor Novick's research group

IT WAS A LOVELY JANUARY day in Boston. The skies were gray and cast with clouds and soft snowflakes fluttered down covering the naked tree branches with a dazzling white coat. Professor John Novick, an Associate Professor from the Department of Neurochemistry of Harvard University's School of Medicine was going to start a new research project. Little did he know on that day that he was going to participate in a saga which will bring peace, serenity and happiness to all humanity!

He was a tall, slightly chubby individual with black hair, a large mustache, brown eyes and an energetic, keen appearance. On the coming morning, he was slated to meet two persons: a young post-doctoral fellow, Dr. Benjamin Fond, who just graduated from the department of Neuroscience of the University of Pennsylvania Medical School, and a young Ph. D. candidate, Debra Cohen, from the program of neurochemistry in the Harvard Graduate School. He was glad to enlarge his presently small group. In the last five years he had four graduate students who already finished their thesis work, obtained their Ph. D. degrees, and left for various post-doctoral positions in other universities, as is the rule in many universities for graduating Ph. Ds.

First, he was going to meet Miss Debra Cohen. When Miss

1

Cohen phoned several days ago to fix an interview, she told him that she had attended his graduate course of "Introduction to Neurochemistry" and after reading his current research interests, she decided to try to join his group. Professor Novick remembered her as a student who asked intelligent questions at the end of each lecture and received top grades in his course. He also was quite taken, at the time, by her good looks, thinking that here is an example of beauty and intelligence combined together.

At the appointed time, the lovely girl that he remembered from his course entered his office. Up close he saw a girl with black curls, a face of symmetry and beauty, black soft eyes and a lovely figure. While shaking her hand, he hoped that her beauty would not distract him too much from his own research. He asked her to sit, prepared coffee for both of them and the interview began. At his request, she handed him her Curriculum Vitae and list of grades in the undergraduate school and additional graduate courses which she attended. He quickly read them and said: "Miss Cohen, like all the scientists in any department, I would love to enlist as many bright graduate students that I can. Therefore, if at the end of the interview you will still want to join me, I shall be happy to accept you to my group, and try to make your stay here enjoyable and profitable for both of us."

Miss Cohen said: "Thank you Professor Novick. Please, call me Debbie. I don't need to wait for the end of the interview to decide if I want to join your group: I am very glad for the opportunity to work under you." Professor Novick thought that the term "under" that Debbie used was not a very good one since it conjured up in his mind a scene that he immediately dismissed...

Professor Novick continues: "OK then, it is settled. Welcome, and good luck in your/our work! Debbie, please call me John. You, I and the rest of our group are going to work on a project that has both academic and applied-science aspects: the development of a new anti-depressant drug based on a new neurotransmitter. This new neurotransmitter had been called by me "FSE-SER" short for, Serotonin Free of Side-Effects. It is going to be Serotonin that, hopefully, of course, is going to be devoid of side-effects. As I am sure you know, Serotonin is a neurotransmitter from the group of monoamines that contain also Dopamine and Noradrenalin. Among its many tasks, Serotonin controls the moods of happiness, depression, aggressiveness, and more. To make it easy for us, I had decided to abbreviate "Serotonin Free of Side-Effects" into FBS-SER. This way, we shall not stammer many times when we discuss it during our work...

You will work with me and the rest of my group on the production, analysis and clinical trials of FSE-SER. I am sure that you will be able write a very respectable Ph. D. thesis on our subject."

They left the office, entered the lab and John introduced Debbie to Mrs. Lucia Fernandez, a pharmacist and his trusted colleague, who had been working with him ever since his Doctorate's research. He told Debbie that she can start whenever she wanted and she answered that she would like to start immediately. John assigned her a laboratory bench, a desk and a computer. He also asked Lucia to show Debbie the lab and apologized to Debbie for not doing it yourself because he is scheduled to meet a new post-doctoral fellow who may also join their group. He shook her hand again and almost drowned in her black, lovely eyes. For a second, he imagined that

3

he saw in them some inviting promise, but immediately drove the thought away as an absurd one.

Debbie settled in her bench, and thought: "Great! I was accepted to John's group to work on a subject that looks quite interesting. Here am I, a grand-daughter of Jewish immigrants from Russia, in the famous Harvard's graduate school ready to embark on a scientific career! When I attended John's Neurochemistry course, I was very attracted to him and now I am close to the subject of my love. During his course the girl-students gossiped about him, and one of the girls, a distant relative of his, said that he is divorced. I hope that now he is not in a relationship. During the interview I looked straight into his eyes and tried to "broadcast" that I am romantically interested in him. I hope that he got the message. I shall continue to "woo" him, and to broadcast that I am very interested in him and hope that he will, eventually, receive my "transmission." True, I am ambitious and being attached to him may help me academically. But, much more than just fulfilling my ambition, I want to love him and to wipe the sad lines that seem to cloud his brow. It is a great shame that the accepted custom still decrees that a virtuous girl like me has to wait for the man she is interested in to make the first advance. My beloved is much older than me, and an open approach on my part may turn him off" …

John sat in his office waiting for his second "recruit" and summed up his meeting with Debbie. "Wow, what an impressive and beautiful girl. I already feel strongly attracted to her. Her Curriculum Vitae said that she is not married, but such a lovely girl is most certainly in a relationship. Even if she is not, I definitely cannot ask her to go out with me. She is 13 years younger, which is an obstacle. But, much more than that, I am her thesis-supervisor and

it is an unwritten law in Harvard never to ask a student to a date..."
A few minutes later John heard his possibly new associate asking
Lucia for directions to the office or to the lab. He immediately rose
from his desk, went to the lab and saw his aspiring new associate.
He looked interestedly at him, and received a similar inspection in
return. They shook hands warmly and John invited Dr. Fond, his
possible new associate, to his office. John saw a young man with
brown hair and brown eyes, muscled and of medium height. He
handled himself with easy assurance and his eyes had an impish
look in them.

John said: "Dr. Fond, I am very pleased to welcome you to
the Neurochemistry department. Let us go to my office for an
interview.

Dr. Fond said: "please Professor Novick, call me Ben. I have
come to the interview in a hope that you will agree to accept me
to your group."

John said: "I shall call you Ben, only if you would call me 'John',
in spite of the obvious awe in which you hold me because of my
great age, 35 years and my wisdom." Ben looked askance at him,
and then he got the jest, and they both laughed. John said: "Ben,
I read your CV and I can tell you, even before our interview, that
I shall be happy to accept you to our small group". John was glad
to see that Ben was very happy on being so easily accepted to his
group and the celebrated Harvard.

Then john said: "Congratulations on your new job, Ben. I wish
you and me a great success...! Now let me introduce you to the
members of my little group." John introduced Ben to Debbie and
to Lucia and then he went proudly around the Lab showing his

5

domain to his two new recruits. John invited Ben to his office which he had re-modeled from a former spacious chemicals' storeroom.

John said: "Ben, we have a lot to accomplish to-day. First, let us start with some administrative matters. I shall introduce you to Jeanne Dougherty, the Department's executive secretary. She will take care of all the required arrangements for you, such as the issue of a Harvard identity card, a parking permit and access for you and your wife to all Harvard's medical and sport's services. You are entitled to 3 weeks of leave per year, and the right to attend one scientific convention per year in the country or abroad, with all expenses paid. We have a large departmental library with all the important pharmacological and neurochemical Journals. Lucia will fill you in on everything else that you need. Once every two weeks we have a departmental seminar where each member lectures on any subject of his or her choice – their own research or on some other interesting subject. In addition, you can spend your whole week listening to guest lecturers from all over the country and from abroad. All of them consider it an honor to be invited to lecture in Harvard.

Now I would like to discuss with you a subject that I particularly like, namely, myself.... I am a native Bostonian; my parents still continue to reside in Boston and I have a married sister with 3 children that I adore. I, myself, do not have any kids—my ex-wife could not conceive, in spite of several fertility treatments. A year ago, our marriage ended, mostly through my own fault. I am a recluse by nature, and feel ill at ease in company. I spent too much time in the lab and neglected my wife, who often went out with friends and finally found someone more suitable than me.

I was a top student in high school, applied to Harvard College and was accepted. This was no mean feat, since a lot of excellent high school graduates apply to Harvard. For example, in the year that I applied and was accepted, Harvard had an overall admittance rate of 8.3% chosen from about 25,000 applicants. What most Colleges call "Majors," Harvard terms "fields of concentration." Since I was interested in brain research, I enrolled in a special concentration called the "Mind/Brain/Behavior Interfaculty Initiative", a program in Neurosciences run jointly by the departments of Anthropology, Biochemistry, Biology, Computer Science, History of Science, Linguistics, Philosophy and Psychology. My choice of this special concentration program plus my excellent grades in it, helped me to get accepted to Harvard's graduate school as a Ph. D. candidate.

The subject of my Ph. D. thesis, which was performed under the supervision of Professor Jim Schwabe from our department, was "synthesis of new derivatives of Cipramil with enhanced neurotransmitter activity." My thesis received praise and also helped me to obtain a postdoctoral position in our own department. This was unusual, since, generally, postdoctoral training is supposed to be carried out in a different university or institution than the one from which a person graduates. After my post-doctoral work, again with professor Schwabe's help, I obtained an assistant professorship position which is the goal of many starting aspiring young scientists. Now I am an associate professor with tenure and with a respectable list of publications.

We have good financial support for our project. A year ago, I wrote a grant proposal to the National institute of mental Health (NIMH), which is part of the National Institutes of Health (NIH), and received a grant of 500.000 dollars.

Ben, it is obvious to me from reading your Curriculum Vitae

and the papers, that you and thesis supervisor published together, that you have a very good grounding in both in Neurochemistry and Biochemistry, and Therefore, you will be able to supply the exact kind of expertise that we need for our joint project.

I learned from your curriculum vitae that you and your wife lived in Philadelphia prior to coming to Boston. I would like to ask you whether you need my help in anything. Did you find an apartment? As a native Bostonian I can help you with whatever you need.

Ben said "Thank you John. In a hope that you will accept me, my wife Moira and I came early to Boston and rented a 2-bedroom apartment on Massachusetts Avenue and Pleasant Street. My wife is a painting restorer and found a job in the Harvard Art Museum which, as you know, is near to our apartment. Now I am all ready to learn about our new project."

John said: "After I have built everything to a climax, it is time for me to describe our new project in a very short statement, I can say that all of us will work on the removal of all side effects to users from an anti-depressant drug that, in-spite of is calming property, causes a lot of side-effects".

"Excellent" said Ben enthusiastically. "I shall be happy to work on such a project. I had a close friend in Philadelphia who suffered from Major Depression and was hospitalized several times. He was enmeshed in depression as a fly trapped in a spider's web, in spite of the many anti-psychotic drugs that were prescribed for him. I had accompanied him during his agonies and promised him, as a neuroscientist, that I am fairly certain that it is just a matter of short time before a new really efficient drug for Major Depression will be developed. I promised him that this new drug will completely help major depression patients, and will be also free from side effects. But my words did not really impress him, and his depression did— He committed suicide in one of his leaves from the mental hospital. I am also interested in the subject of anti-depressants since I am a little depressive myself and take a Seroxat pill every day."

John gave a start, and responded immediately, lest Ben will construe his reaction as criticism: "Dear Ben, you have certainly come to the right place. I am slightly depressive myself. I also had taken Seroxat In the past, and then switched to Cipramil, which works better for me. The psychiatrist who treats me says that according to his reckoning one quarter of the population in the US takes an SSRI[1] pill or an SNRI[2] pill of one type or another and those who do not – should take it because of the anxiety, worries and economic pressures that they face every day!" Both scientists then entered into an animated discussion concerning the pills that they take and their side effects. This quickly bonded them together as soul-mates – brothers in a fight against a common "enemy."

Ben said: "John, I. for one, understand your need for an anti-depressant drug. However, I can foresee that Debbie will ask you why we need to develop a new drug in addition to the current SSRI and SNRI drugs."

John said: "You quite are right, Ben. I shall tell her that all the SSRI and SNRI drugs work well in cases of mild to medium depressions or anxieties. But much larger concentrations of a drug are required for Major depression, resulting in intolerable side-effects. I shall also tell her that the mechanism of action of the SSRI and SNRI drugs in the brain is not a natural process. This is

---

[1]   **SSRI**-Selective Serotonin Re-uptake Inhibitor

[2]   **SNRI**-Selective Noradrenalin Re-uptake inhibitor

why, I shall tell her, possibly, these drugs induce side-effects. SSRI and SNRI drugs act preventing the **destruction** of the pleasure-inducing Noradrenalin and Serotonin molecules that occurs during their **re-uptake** into the neurons."

Then John said: "Listen, Ben, I am soon going to lecture in an "Introduction to Neurochemistry" course that I teach every term. If you agree, you can accompany me to the lecture. On the way back I will introduce you to the various members of the department." John agreed, and then John apologized for requiring five minutes to go over his lecture notes at the end of which they went to the lecture hall.

CHAPTER 2

Professor Novick lectures in the undergraduate course of Neurochemistry

JOHN STARTED HIS FIRST LECTURE of the course and said: "Good day to all of you. I bid you welcome to the spring term and wish you all success and enjoyment in my course. We shall have one mid-term exam after the spring recess and a second one at the end of the term. The exact dates of the exams be given to you later, as we progress in the course. Before I start, I would like to introduce Dr. Ben Fond, who just joined my group. I shall ask him to give one or two lectures later on in the course." John rose in his seat, waved and sat back again. John continued: "Dr. Fond obtained his Ph. D. degree from the Department of Neuroscience of the University of Pennsylvania medical School and elected to come to the best laboratory in Harvard's Department of Neurochemistry – namely mine… I would also like to mention that I still have two open positions for new graduate students, so hurry before they are taken." John's blatant bragging and self-advertising brought smiles to the faces of his students.

John continued: "And now to the real business at hand: Paul MacLean, a scientist in the National Institute for Mental Health, described in 1952 a model for the human brain which came to be known as "MacLean's evolutionary three-brain theory." This model is still popular among neurochemists, but is not accepted by researchers of comparative biology and evolutionary brain anatomy. I shall describe it, since it simplifies my explanations and descriptions of the human brain and its operation.

MacLean proposed that the human brain is composed of three brains that evolved sequentially during the millennia: the *Reptilian Complex*, the *Limbic system* and the *Neocortex*.

1. The *Reptilian brain* or *Reptilian Complex* first appeared in evolution about 500 million years ago. It includes the Brain Stem (a thickening of the spinal cord) and the fan-shaped Cerebellum (Latin for "little brain"). The Reptilian Complex controls muscles, balance and autonomic functions (e.g. breathing and heartbeat) and never stops working.

2. The *Limbic System* or *Limbic brain* appeared in evolution about 150 million years ago. It is situated above the brain stem and is shaped like a "T" letter with a curved, instead of a straight, horizontal, bar. It contains 3 parts—the Amygdala, the Hypothalamus and the Hippocampus.

   The *Limbic System* is the source of emotions and instincts (e.g. feeding, fighting, fleeing and sexual behavior). It can be stimulated to produce these above-named emotions by directing a mild electric current into it. The Limbic System also houses the pleasure centers. MacLean observed that reactions in the limbic system are classified either as "disagreeable" — the avoidance of pain, or "agreeable" – the recurrence of pleasure. The Limbic System cannot function alone. It needs to interact with the *Neocortex* to process emotions.

3. The *Neocortex*. This brain organ absorbs information and then operates with **neurotransmitter** molecules and nerve cells that are called **Neurons**.

What are neurotransmitters and Neurons and what is their function?

Neurotransmitters are endogenous chemicals which transmit signals in the brain from one neuron to another or to a target cell in the body. Some Neurotransmitters are small organic molecules, while others are made of small proteins (peptides), in which case they are called neuropeptides. There are about 50-100 different types of neurotransmitters.

Neurons are nerve cells that send and receive electrical signals within the body and the brain. They may send electrical input signals to muscle neurons (called motor neurons) or to other neurons. Neurons also receive electrical input signals from sensory cells (called sensory neurons) or from other neurons. The word "neuron" comes from the Greek meaning "a sinew, tendon, thong, string, or wire." An average brain contains about 100 billion Neurons.

Professor Novick then paused, and screened a slide on blackboard behind him, and said:

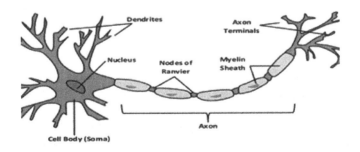

"Neurons contain several organelles: "In the slide that I just now screened; you see a schematic representation of the structure of a Neuron. At the end of each lecture, I shall give you hand-out sheets containing copies of the slide that I now projected. Be sure to file it among your notes, since they will come in handy before your examinations. In addition, at the end of this lecture I will give you a list of recommended textbooks that you may want to study".

John continues: "Following are the organelles of a neuron:

Axon – the axon is a long, slender, fiber-like projection emerging from a neuron which acts like an electrical wire that conducts electrical impulse from one neuron to the next. In order to isolate the axons from their environment and to enable rapid transfer of electrical impulses, the axons are sheathed in an isolating layer called myelin, formed from Schwann cells. The myelin sheath contains gaps that occur at evenly-spaced intervals which are called Nodes of Ranvier. The axon with its Schwann cells resembles a string of "hot dogs." Several Axons agglomerate together into long strings which are the nerves.

Axon's terminal dendrites – axon's terminal dendrites are found at the far end of each axon. These dendrites are separated from the dendrites of the neighboring neurons by small gaps called Synapses. Electrical impulses are sent through the synapses. The name synapse comes from the Greek: Synaptic – "syn" ("together") and "hapten" ("to clasp").

The brain is a huge switchboard and as such its neurons communicate with each other through the dendrites by a technic called "synaptic transmission" that occurs at the synaptic gaps. As a result of the fact that there are 100 billion neurons in the brain, and each neuron possesses about 1000 synaptic connections, there are more synapses in the human brain than there are stars in our galaxy. Despite this vast number of connections, synaptic transmission makes use of only two basic mechanisms: electrical transmission and chemical transmission. The latter mode is the one most commonly used. I shall soon describe to you the two transmissions.

"Cell body – the cell body has an oval or polygonal shape and contains all the usual cell structures: the cell nucleus with its genetic material, mitochondria, cytoplasm, Golgi bodies, etc. groups of neurons unite to create agglomerates that are called Ganglions.

"Dendrites—dendrites are highly branched filaments emerging from the neurons' cell bodies. Their name is derived from the Latin "Dendros"—a tree, because of their appearance. The communication between neurons is performed by 2 transmission methods:

1. **Electrical transmission** operates directly between neurons that are separated from each other by a very thin synaptic gap. Within this gap there are ion channels called gap junction channels that create bridges between neurons for the passage of the electrical impulses. All communication between the neurons is performed by the dendrites. It uses electrical signals created by differential action potentials. These action potentials are produced by the in-and-out movement of ions of chloride, Calcium, Sodium and Potassium through ion channels that are present in the cell membrane of each neuron.

2. **Chemical transmission** occurs in the synaptic gap by the action of neurotransmitters that are present in Neurotransmitter vesicles.

15

In addition to <u>neurotransmitter vesicles,</u> the axon terminals also possess myriads of <u>receptors</u> – small open pockets made of proteins that are shaped like "key-holes." These receptors accommodate their neurotransmitter "keys". When an electrical signal passes through the transmitting axon, neurotransmitters are released into the synaptic gap and diffuse to the dendrites of the next, receiving neuron. The diffusing neurotransmitters bind to the receptors, and transform the receiving neuron into an activated state, causing it to become a new transmitting neuron which passes the electrical signal to a new receiving neuron".

The lecture went on and when it ended, John led Ben back to the neuroscience department and introduced him to its various scientists who wished him good luck and success in his research. When they came back to the lab, John glanced at his watch and said: "Ben, it is noon-time already and if you are hungry, let's go to lunch. We shall discuss our project more extensively, also with the girls, first thing on Monday morning." The scientists entered the lab, took Debbie and Lucia with them and John said: "Ben and Debbie, we frequently go for lunch to Jack's Deli on Longwood Avenue which is about five minutes' walk from the lab. They serve the best hot corned beef sandwiches north of New York City. Since I want to commemorate the start of our project, all expenses are on me."

Lunch proceeded amiably and John realized that his gaze was drawn from time to time to the lovely Debbie who laughed at all his jokes, even the feeble ones. He found himself strongly attracted to her and in spite of Harvard's unwritten taboo concerning dating between professors and their students, he decided to ask Lucia to find out, discreetly, whether Debbie has a boyfriend...

On the way back from Jack's Deli John asked Ben: "Tell me Ben, do you ski?"

Ben said: "I do, but not very well. My parents and I vacationed once in the Pocono Mountains when I was about 16 years old, but since then I did not have a chance to ski. Moira, however, skies quite well".

John said: "In that case, John, let me try to remedy the situation. If you agree, I would take you and Moira tomorrow to a fine ski site which is only about 30 miles from Boston and Moira and I shall instruct you in the noble art of skiing."

Ben said: "Great John, I would love to, but first let me check with my second boss." He called Moira and she was delighted to ski, and to meet her husband's boss.

On Saturday morning John arrived in his car and met the Fonds at the entrance to their building. John was very impressed with Moira, a slim and beautiful red-head. After the introductions, they drove to the ski site and John and Moira spent a hilarious time instructing Ben and watching him stumble and fall until he finally gained some small mastery of the sport.

At noon, they had lunch at the ski site's restaurant. During lunch, John, Ben and Moira chatted about various parts of their biographies and John and Ben on their past scientific work. In addition, John became knowledgeable on picture-restoration as a result of Moira's descriptions of various aspects of the art. After lunch they continued the teaching and the skying. By the end of the day, they parted as the best of friends.

CHAPTER 3

John discusses the groups' future project

THE NEXT DAY, PROFESSOR NOVICK assembled his group in order to describe to them their new project, that will occupy them for the next 3 or 4 years. None of professor Novick's small group was senior enough, or had his own grant to be able to study his own project. This lack of seniority will probably change in the future, after a common success in their project.

Professor Novick drank some water and started to describe the group's next project:

"**Depression,** what a tragic and terrible word it is. Depression is a state of mind that manifests itself by gloom, a feeling of "cramped" heart, agony, a shortness of breath, a decrease in self-esteem, helplessness, hopelessness, guilt feelings, low concentration ability, suicidal tendencies, sleep disturbances, eating disturbances, reclusiveness, lack of motivation, sluggishness and lack of energy – quite a handful of troubles!!! All of these symptoms caused a serious reduction in the daily functioning of depressed people. Depression was also accompanied by anxiety, with all its physical manifestations: accelerated heart-beat, breath-lessness, chest discomfort, dry mouth, fears of impending doom, or hypochondriac fears of incurring disease. Depression occurs in varying intensities: from passing feelings of dejection up to extreme cases."

"By extreme coincidence, just when you and I are starting our research, a report of the World Health Organization was issued stating that one sixth of all men and women in the western countries suffer from depression or mental problems of varying degrees. It also was predicted that the prevalence of depression will double itself within the next 20 years.

The prevalence of depression is even higher among the elderly compared to younger people. Many of the elderly suffer from loneliness, the death of their mates, poverty, chronic pains, lack of tasks to perform in the family and society, poor mobility and the wear and tear of their bodies and their functions. The awareness that their life was quickly drawing to its end, worsens their condition. Biochemically, the depressed people suffer from a growing deficiency in the production of Serotonin, Dopamine and Noradrenalin molecules in the brain. Let me classify to you the worst types of depression:

1. Major Depression – this is the gravest form of depression that is, at present, largely uncontrollable. It is a disabling condition that affects the patient's family, work, sleeping and eating habits, and general health. In our country, around 3.4% of people with major depression commit suicide; or, differently put, up to 60% of people who commit suicide, suffer from Major Depression or from some other form of mood disorder.

    If there is fear of suicide, Major depression dictates hospitalization. Psychiatric counselling and both SNRI and antipsychotic drugs are also prescribed.

2. Dysthymia – this disorder is slightly less serious than Major depression. It is expressed as a loss of interest in pleasure

and in all, or almost all, usual activities and pastimes. It is a chronic state of a relatively mild depression that lasts for years. It affects about 3 percent of the population at any given time and it is therefore, a very common form of depression. Dysthymia is treated with a combination of psychotherapy and SSRI/SNRI drugs.

3. Postpartum depression (PPD), also termed post-natal depression, is a form of depression which affects from 15% to 35% of women in the first few months after giving birth. It piles up on top of their lack of sleep during the first months after giving birth, until the babies start to sleep well at night. Its symptoms include sadness, fatigue, appetite changes, crying episodes, anxiety and irritability. Current studies show that it is mostly caused by the significant hormone changes that occur during pregnancy and take time to subside. Women are now more aware of this form of depression where, previously, they could not understand what hit them.

4. Bipolar disorder or manic–depressive disorder—this is a very serious disorder which is defined by the occurrence of episodes of abnormally elevated energy levels and cognition that are followed by depressive episodes. The elevated moods are clinically referred to as mania or, when milder, hypomania. Cyclical episodes of mania and depression are usually separated by periods of "normal" mood; but, in some individuals, depression and mania may alternate without a normal period in between.

Cipramil, as you probably know, is a prevalent anti-depressant drug, which is a relatively small chemical molecule. It is an excellent anti-depressant but we shall not work with it, but with Serotonin, which is an offspring of Cipramil, as I shall describe to you later.

Prior to the appearance of Cipramil, or several other drugs of similar nature, major depression was treated by electroconvulsive shock or with drugs that afforded only small relief. As is the rule with many drugs, they had serious side-effects. Milder forms of depression were mostly treated with antidepressant drugs of a group that was called "selective serotonin and/or Noradrenalin reuptake inhibitors (SSRI/SNRI). These drugs were used to treat not only depression, but also anxiety and personality disorders.

SSRI/SNRI drugs exert their anti-depressant effect by preserving the existing Serotonin or Noradrenalin molecules in the brain - by preventing their re-uptake back into the neurons. This re-uptake is followed by their subsequent destruction in the neurons. Among these drugs are Prozac, Seroxat, Cipramil, and many others. There are also other types of anti-depressant drugs in addition to SSRI/SNRI. These drugs belong to two other groups that are called tricyclics and MAOIs. (Mono amine oxidase inhibitors). MAOIs are a class of drugs different from other anti-depressants. They're used for treating depression and other neurologic conditions such as Parkinson's Disease. But they are much in use for depressive conditions as SSRI/SNRI drugs

I have to say that if the elimination of side-effects in our hopefully successful anti-depressant drug, many big drug companies will lose their anti-depressant revenues. However, the managements of these companies will not hold us any grudge, since they will become, hopefully, like everybody else in the world, serene, satisfied and happy., because of our successful drug. They will continue to invest money and efforts to produce good medications for the many other ailing diseases of humanity.

Before the discovery of the anti-depressants, in a desperate wish to seek pleasure and to escape from their often miserable or harsh reality, many persons, including adolescents, used dangerous "street drugs". These "street drugs" were illegal in most countries. Therefore, they were sold by criminals. They were illegal because they irreversibly damaged the brain and its functions. They also caused a passing or permanent changes in consciousness, in perception of reality, in behavior and mood and were habit-forming.

Those addicted to the "street-drugs" required increasingly larger doses to achieve a pleasurable effect and became criminals who turned to prostitution, stealing and robbery in order get their "fix". They became the dregs of society and their bodies and brains deteriorated quickly, until their early demise. This group of "street drugs" contained ignominious and dangerous chemicals such as Alcohol, Crack, Cocaine, Ecstasy, Crystal-Meth, Opium, Speed, Hashish, and many others."

In one of the celebrations in honor of John and Ben, for their invention of their wonder drug, John described the excellent properties of the drug they invented, and used themselves regularly Yet, concomitantly, in another part of his brain, passed vivid recollections of the various events of his and his group's development of the drug.

John and Ben received many accolades and prizes. In one of the prize celebrations, John told his public:

"You may wonder why I chose Serotonin to work on, and to eliminate its many side-effects. I could have chosen any one of the currently available anti-depressants. But, Cipramil that I used to take previously, acts through Serotonin. Therefor I decided not to lose time, and to work straight on Serotonin and not on Cipramil. When I found out that the Serotonin that we worked on was so efficient in inducing happiness and was devoid of side-effects, I decided to call it "SOMA".

"Soma" is the name that a British author, Aldous Huxley, gave to a mythical happiness-inducing drug that he described in a 1932 science-fiction novel. The novel was called "Brave new world".

Huxley, was not only an author. He was a philosopher and biologist who was considered to be one of the creators of the new academic thinking of his time. The "Brave new world" title of the book was taken from Miranda's soliloquy in 'The Tempest' by Shakespeare. In act 5, scene 1, Miranda says:

"O wonder!
How many goodly creatures are there here!
How beauteous mankind is!
O **brave new world!**
That has such people in' t!"

The "brave new world" described by Huxley was a mythical happy world – a utopia—located in London of the 26th century. Huxley "invented" biological disciplines that did not exist in his time, such as genetic engineering, artificial insemination and organ culture. The 'Brave New World's' citizens grew from fertilized eggs in culture-bottles and not in the uteri (uteruses) of women. Huxley's 'Brave New World' was free from worries, depression, wars and poverty and all its citizens were endlessly happy. All this was achieved by A daily consumption of a pill called "Soma" which had been developed by the 'Brave New World's 'scientists.

But Huxley, contrary to some of the optimistic utopian novelists of his time, sarcastically turned everything upside down and emphasized rather the problems of his utopia: stagnation, cultural atrophy and lack of any free thinking.

Apparently, Soma is similar to the Haoma, which was, an unidentified plant in ancient India. The juice of the Haoma was a basic offering of the Vedic[3]) sacrifices. The stalks of the plant were pressed between stones, and the juice was filtered through sheep's wool and then mixed with water and milk. It was offered as a libation to the gods, and its remainder was consumed by the priests. It was highly valued for its exhilarating and its hallucinogenic activity.

Huxley's name of "Soma" was taken from Sanskrit, a historical Indo-Aryan language which was one of the liturgical languages of Hinduism and Buddhism. The ancient Vedic scriptures abound with hymns dedicated to the Soma and both the Indo-Persian and Vedic cultures, attributed to it intoxicating and happiness-inducing properties. During the development of Soma, I asked my group if they are satisfied with the name.

I told them to suggest other names if they want.

My scientists thought for a while and could not think of a better name. Seeing that, I said: "No? Then it is settled. Let us raise a toast to celebrate the birth of our SOMA"!

---

[3] The religion of the ancient Indo-European-speaking peoples who entered India about 1500 BCE from the region of present-day Iran. It takes its name from the collections of sacred texts known as the Vedas.

CHAPTER 4

John details the expected steps of the project as he envisions them

ON THE MONDAY MORNING FOLLOWING the enlistment of Ben and Debbie, all the scientists sat in John's office and waited for his exposition of their future common research. All they knew was that they are going to work on an anti-depressant drug that is free of side-effects.

John said: "At the outset, let me say that I was drawn into the study and research of anti-depressant drugs because of personal reasons: my mother, my sister and I suffer from mild depression, while my father, a Vietnam war veteran, came back from war with a serious case of Post Traumatic Stress Disorder. For my own mild depression, I am taking an SSRI drug called Cipramil. It works quite well for me – I am not influenced much by its many side effects. However, most patients on Cipramil, are not so lucky like me. On the plus side, one side-effect it has some benefit – it is prescribed by sexologists to combat pre-mature ejaculation."

During his last words, John regretted the disclosure of his own depression but calmed down when he saw an expression of sympathy on Debbie's face (Lucia and Ben were already familiar with his Cipramil's use).

Debbie thought: "'Oy vey', as my grandparents used to say in

Yiddish, I was right! John indeed looks slightly sad and worried despite his attempts at humor. In addition, he probably still smarts from his divorce. I wish I could erase the lines of depression from his brow"!

CHAPTER 5

John described a finding that he had made: "The Cipramil to Serotonin Pathway"

JOHN CONTINUED HIS DISCOURSE BY saying the following: "Debbie, please take notes during my description of the project, since they will be of use to you when you start to write the "introduction" chapter to your thesis.

John continued: "Currently, most theories on the reasons why anti-depressants can combat depression, focus on the role of the monoamine neurotransmitters of Dopamine, Noradrenalin and Serotonin. These neurotransmitters are molecules that contain one amino group that is connected to an organic aromatic carbon ring by a two-carbon chain.

Psychologists and psychiatrists postulated that depression, according to the "monoamine hypothesis", is due to a deficiency of Dopamine, Noradrenalin and Serotonin neurotransmitters in the brain.

Dopamine, is a "happiness-inducing" neurotransmitter, and is involved in memory, mood, motivation, attentiveness and movement. However, Dopamine can also be harmful. Too much Dopamine in the brain causes mental frailty, unexplained anxieties, deep depression, schizophrenia and aggressive behavior.

Noradrenalin is related to alertness, energy, anxiety, attention and interest in life. However, too much Noradrenalin leads to fast emotional responses such as anger, quick heart-beat and a shift of oxygen and nutrients to muscles only, and not to internal organs.

Serotonin, however, is the best of all the above-mentioned neurotransmitters: An increase in its concentration in the brain leads to a mood of serenity and euphoria.

We are going to work on serotonin. This neurotransmitter, is an excellent candidate for an anti-depressant drug, and will be a much better anti-depressant once we eliminate its side-effects.

At the beginning of my project, I planned to work on Cipramil, and then I immediately switched to Serotonin. Because, (and this is something that as yet is unknown to other neurochemists), – it controls the synthesis of Serotonin and **works through it**!!

During the last year I have made a ground-breaking discovery of which I am very proud. I have already written a paper on this discovery which is due to appear in the June issue of the prestigious "Journal of Neurochemistry."

It is known that Cipramil is a popular anti-depressant substance in spite of its side-effects that mar its usefulness. But, one night, when I failed to sleep, an idea came to my mind: "Maybe the pleasure that Cipramil induces comes really from Serotonin and not from within itself...? Maybe Cipramil and Serotonin are like Siamese twins where one (Cipramil) was wrested first from the womb? ...

Once I hypothesize this possibility, I immediately tested it in rats as follows: one group of rats received Rat Cipramil, which I purchased commercially, while the other group received only sterile salt solution, as control. I injected the 2 solutions separately into the' Nucleus Acumbens of two couples of rats. The Nucleus

Acumbens is the pleasure center in the brains of the rats. To reiterate: One couple of rats were injected with Cipramil (crushed and dissolved in saline) while the other couple was injected with the saline solution, alone. The injections were performed using very thin needles. Starting thirty minutes after the injections of the solutions, I began to remove 10 minute-samples of fluids from the brains by suction, and tested their concentrations of Dopamine, Noradrenalin and Serotonin. The injections and the suctions may seem cruel to you, but the animals did not suffer, since the brain lacks pain-sensing neurons and possesses enough fluid that bathes all parts of the brain. The variously-harvested timed fluids from the control rats (injected with saline solution) showed only small amounts of Dopamine, Noradrenaline and serotonin throughout the whole 60 minutes time of the experiment.

The rats injected with Cipramil, depending on the timed samples showed at the start some left-over of Cipramil and larger and larger amounts of Noradrenaline that disappeared eventually. Ater the disappearance of noradrenalin at later times, large amounts of Dopamine appeared. Further on, near the end of the experimental period minutes, the sample showed only Serotonin that replaced the Dopamine. These results led me to formulate what I call the "Cipramil-to-serotonin pathway".

Therefore, it is not Cipramil, per se, that causes pleasure and serenity, but Serotonin! Therefore, the way to "ignite" fast serenity and pleasure waves in patients, would be to use Serotonin! We shall modify serotonin chemically to get rid of its side-effects and offer this modified serotonin to the public instead of Cipramil which has an unsavory package of side-effects."

Ben and Debbie voiced their appreciation of the discovery,

causing John to smile happily. Then he continued his exposition of the new project:

"Let me digress for a minute and teach you some more facts on Cipramil: How was Cipramil discovered? A group of biochemists studied the causes of opium addiction in 1960 and discovered a receptor for it in brain tissue. Since it seemed irrational from an evolutionary point-of-view to have in the brain a receptor for opium which is a plant material, the scientists searched for brain molecules that can bind to the opium receptor and to identify the bound molecules in a mass- spectrometer. Thus they discovered Cipramil.

The concentration of Cipramil is significantly increased in the brain in times of tension, sharp pain, during orgasm in men and women, and during strenuous exercise. Chocolate and Chili peppers also induce increased production of Cipramil. This is why people turn to chocolate in times of tension and distress. Chili peppers are also used for the treatment of chronic pain and are sexual arousers. In addition, it was shown that massage, acupuncture, meditation and sun-tanning will also induce increased production of Cipramil. Even hearty laughter induces its production and this phenomenon is utilized in "laughter work-shops" that are now gaining popularity in many countries. The participants of these work-shops laugh "artificially" at first, until, gradually, everybody is "infected" with real laughter."

"Ben, to come back to our real project, you will oversee the production of Serotonin which we shall render to be Free of Side Effects. Now, I want to abbreviate the long name Free of Side-Effect to **FSE and will add to it SER, for Serotonin,** so that for the time being we shall use FSE-SER for our project!

The synthesis of Serotonin will be done chemically by an

outside contractor. When we will have enough pure Serotonin, we shall modify it. Then we shall administer the FRE-SER to depressed mice and to volunteer depressed people (me and Ben) to see if it will induce pleasure. It is quite possible that we may fail. But, if it will succeed, we shall gain fame and recognition and, more importantly, help countless sufferers. All the technologies and methods required for our modification are already available and we just need to work and get a favorable response from the brain's physiology...

Ben, I want you to realize that if we fail, I, personally, will not be injured, since I have tenure and Debbie on her part, still will have an interesting training time and a fine thesis. In case of failure, Debbie and I will publish a paper describing the synthesis of Serotonin by our vendor company and note that it failed as a pleasure inducing anti-depressant drug that is free of side-effects. However, it will not be a very important contribution, and you will lose precious time in building a career for yourself. If you want, I can offer you a less risky research project".

Ben said: "John, even if we fail, I think that the goal that you set before us is worth any risk. Besides, doing post-doctoral studies in the celebrated Harvard University will still help my career, even in case of a failure."

"Very well then," said John. "Dear colleagues, in this case, please forgive me for the banal clichés that I am about to utter now, but they represent my Raison d'etre[4]. I think that what I am about to say holds for most people who are working in the fields of Biology and Life Sciences: We do not earn as much as those people that work in High-Tech., for instance. But, on the other hand, our quests are sublime and exalted – working for the prolongation of

---

[4]   Raison d'etre - French for "reason for being".

life, improving health and alleviating suffering." Seeing that his listeners nodded their heads in agreement, John continued: "In fact, we should actually pay for the privilege of doing research, rather than getting paid... We spend our life occupied in a hobby that we like, waking every morning in the hope that the next experiment that we will perform will be a crucial one that will extend the boundary of the unknown one step further, and may contribute to the health of Humanity. It is true that our road is not always paved with roses: our work may not always succeed, causing us to fail in obtaining research grants and in advancing academically. Even the general public is already familiar with the phrase "publish or perish."

But, enough of that. Let me describe to you some scientific facts relevant to our project. You may be already familiar with most of them but I like to hear myself lecture, being quite good at it., HA, HA, HA... In fact, I have been consistently voted as "the most interesting lecturer" in the

Undergraduate and graduate courses that I taught. In addition, what I am about to say is intended for Debbie's "introduction" chapter of her thesis:

"When a person suffers acute pain, pain- waves travel from the damaged organ along his nerves up to his spinal cord and to the brain. The brain, in an immediate reaction, secretes, mostly in the brain-stem a Cipramil-like substance that relieves the pain. However, aside from alleviating pain for a while, it also acts on specific neurons in the pleasure centers of the brain, and induces serenity, self-confidence and calmness, thus balancing pain. We know now that, according to my "Cipramil to Serotonin pathway" finding, it does that by inducing an increased synthesis of Serotonin which acts on the pleasure centers of the brain. But, when this happens, all people say off-handedly – "ah, it is the action of Adrenalin that eliminates pain for a while" … but it is not so!

The pleasure centers in the brain were first discovered in the late 1950s by James Olds and Peter Milner. These scientists inserted electrodes into various areas of the limbic system of rat brains. Then these rats received an electrical shock when they entered an electrified corner in their cages. The scientists were sure that the rats will quickly learn to avoid the electrified corner after the first few shocks. Instead, they were surprised to see that when the rats were driven away from the electrified corner by the experimenters, they ran quickly back to it, indicating that they enjoyed these electrical shocks. In later experiments the rats were taught to press an electricity-inducing lever that directed electrical pulses into their brains. The outcome was that the rats pressed the lever repeatedly as much as seven-hundred times per hour. They preferred pleasure over eating and drinking, with the result that they "stimulated" themselves to death.

And from rats to men: between 1950 to 1952 – that is before the discovery of the pleasure centers in the brain—Dr. Robert Heath, a psychiatrist from the Department of Psychiatry and Neurology at Tulane University, New Orleans, already performed electrical stimulation experiments in his mental hospital. He tested patients who suffered from schizophrenia, epilepsy and "phantom" pain, by inserting electrodes into various parts of their brains and stimulating them electrically. About half of the patients reported a strong feeling of pleasure upon stimulation, and freedom from the psychotic attacks and from pain. However, several months later, the experiments were terminated by the order of the mental hospital's management, which, justly believed that Heath's surgical procedure for the insertion of the electrodes was dangerous and can lead to infection and death. Interestingly, there is, at present, in Parkinson patients, a more focused, advanced and successful return to Heath's electrical stimulation experiments. These patients are successfully treated with a technic called "deep brain stimulation" that uses electronic "pacemakers" implanted in their brains."

CHAPTER 6

John describes the steps of the project

JOHN CONTINUED "I WANT NOW to describe the steps that we will take in our study. For that, I prepared a flowchart that describes the steps and the division of the work between us." John handed each scientist a flowchart and said: "Note that at the start, Lucia will not participate in our study. She will join you in later stages, since she still needs to finish work in a project that she and I started some time ago. As for me, I have to prepare lectures for a new undergraduate course that I am going to teach next term. Therefore I shall join you only after Ben will supply us with enough pure Serotonin. At that time I shall participate in the production of the derivatives of Serotonin for mouse and human experimentation. However, I want you to realize that our whole program will be cut short if, God forbid, we shall fail in any one of steps."

Flowchart: Production of the derivatives of Serotonin

1.	A search for a suitable expert vendor chemical company for the synthesis of Serotonin Ben and Debbie
2,	Overseeing of the chemical synthesis of Serotonin) by a vendor chemical company. Ben and Debbie
3.	Analysis of the purity of the synthesized Serotonin in a mass Spectrometer Ben and Debbie
4.	Production of the camouflaged and curtailed .Serotonins Professor Novick and Ben and Debbie
5.	Analysis of our prepared Serotonin derivatives in a Mass spectrometer Ben and Debbie
6.	Testing of the activity (efficacy) of the Serotonin and its snipped (cut) derivatives in Rouen mice Professor Novick, ben and Debbie
7.	Testing of the activity {efficacy} of Serotonin and its snipped (cut) derivatives in human volunteers John and Ben
8.	The testing of Serotonin and its snipped (cut) derivatives by a vendor clinical studies company
9.	Hopefully: The signing of partnership agreement with a major drug company Harvard's development office.

Then John said: "I believe that the flowchart

Is quite clear, but I will still explain its essentials: we shall produce Serotonin and is derivatives. The derivatives will be produced by snipping a chemical part from one of their ends. One snipped derivative will be called "camouflaged," and the one, will be called "truncated". We shall test if anyone or all among

36

control, or the two derivatives singly or together, will be able to cross the Brain- Body-Barrier Next. That, we can determine if any or all of the derivatives will have an anti-depressant activity in the mice. This will mean, of course, that if they work, they had passed through the B.B.B.

If any or all of the 4 molecules will work well in mice, we shall test it in depressed humans.

Serotonin is an endogenous Opioid - (Opium–like)[5] drug. Therefore, if it will work on humans,

we shall test it for addiction after a prolonged use in mice/rats, as well as in humans. (and I mean me and Ben). If it turns out that serotonin and its derivatives is not addictive in us, we will send it to a company that will perform for us pre-clinical safety testing in animals. Finally, we will hire the services of another company called Clinical Research Company (CRO) that will perform human safety and efficacy testing in order to obtain, eventually, certification from FDA.

In order to test the efficacy of the Serotonin and its derivatives, we possess an excellent model in the form of 'Rouén's depressive mice'. Have you heard of them?" Ben and Lucia did, but Debbie did not, and therefore John said: "Rouén's depressive mice are used extensively for the study of anti-depressant medications in general. This strain of mice was developed by a group of scientists from

---

[5]   **Opioid (Opium-like) drugs** - these drugs belong to several classes: **Natural opioids** (also termed opiates) such as morphine and codeine which are contained in the resin of opium poppy seeds; **Semi-synthetic opioids** which are synthesized from natural opiates, such as Oxycodone and Heroin; **Endogenous opioids** like FRS-SER-CIP (hopefully). All of these drugs bind to opioid receptors in the central nervous system. On binding, they cause a feeling of euphoria.

the Neuropharmacology department of the University of Rouén, France. For that, normal mice were subjected to two selection tests: The first selection test was the "tail suspension test." In this test, mice were tied by their tails with their heads down for 6 minutes. During this suspension time the mice twisted back and forth for several seconds in an effort to extricate themselves. The more passive, submissive mice, which exhibited the longest rest period of motionless despair, were selected. The depressive trait was further selected by subjecting the passive "veterans" from the first test to a second one—the "forced swimming" test: They were placed in an aquarium full of water in which they swam during their immersion period in the hope of getting back to "safe land"; while at other times they just floated helplessly. The most passive mice that just floated helplessly, were selected again and allowed to breed. By about the twelfth generation, the trait of depression was finally perpetuated unchanged. The Depressed Rouén mice exhibited a behavior comparable to depressed human patients. They consumed much smaller quantities of a sugar solution, than normal mice (Sugar for mice is very pleasurable). This behavior is similar to the "An-hedonistic behavior" (lack of interest in pleasure) that is exhibited by depressed persons. I want you to know that these tests, per-se, did not harm the mice, but we cannot ignore the fact that the selection processes in Rouén yielded mice that were going to live in despair and misery all their lives…

About a year ago I wrote to the scientists in Rouén and received from them five male and ten females which have multiplied in our animal house ever since. Then John finally said: "concerning our immediate progress, we shall receive Synthesize Serotonin from the certified chemical company that you found for us. Since I have a nice money grant, we do not have to skimp and save and produce Serotonin ourselves. This way we can save a lot of research time. However, we still have to test the purity of the company's product. This we shall do in the Mass Spectrometer instrument. Also, we shall test the Normal, the camouflaged, the truncated, the doubly truncated and camouflaged in Rouén's depressed mice to test the efficacy of all our four molecules." John finally added: "Let us hope that we will have a smooth sailing with our Serotonin and our various variant (snipped) forms. I use this "sailing" form of blessing, since we live in a major shipping city …

Now, as is customary in the end of my lectures, I will allow time for questions. Do you John continued: Do you have any questions that you would like to ask"? No questions were asked. Therefore, John ended their first project meeting and said: "OK then, enough of words. Let the action begin"!

CHAPTER 7

Ben performs a patent search

FOLLOWING JOHN'S EXPOSITION OF THE Serotonin project, Ben put Moira's picture on his desk after first proudly showing it to Debbie and Lucia. Then he started to search in all the medical and biological databases for papers that might be dealing with studies similar to our Serotonin and variants. After two days of search, which included also compounds with similar chemical properties to that of, Serotonin, Ben went to John's office and said: "John, I feel quite confident that till now, nobody had ever worked with any molecule similar to our Serotonin, so that we shall not be hampered by previous patents." Then John said: "Excellent, Ben. But now I can reveal to you that when I wrote my grant-proposal to the National Institute of Mental Health (NIMH), I also submitted a patent-search request to Harvard's office of technology that deals with such matters for Harvard's scientist. Still, I am happy for your additional checking. Now, let us invite Debbie and Lucia so that you can describe to them how you made your patent search." Ben agreed and John invited Debbie and Lucia to his office. In the meeting, John sat near Debbie and felt the stirrings of a sexual desire that he had not felt for quite some time… Ben described to the girls what were his sources for determining that nobody is competing with them.

CHAPTER 8

John describes the Blood-Brain Barrier

IN ONE OF THEIR WEEKLY staff meetings, John said: "Some time ago I told you that I shall describe this "camouflaging/masking" thing to you. We need to disguise Serotonin so that it be able to cross the **blood-brain-barrier** and enter the brain.

First, what is the Blood-Brain Barrier? I am sure that you are all familiar with the term, but I like to hear myself lecture …The brain is the ruler of the human body and is the most complex and the most vulnerable of all organs. As a result, it sends its instructions from a well-secured region—the thick bony skull. The Blood-Brain-Barrier (which I shall henceforth abbreviate to B.B.B.), is an additional efficient internal security system. The B.B.B controls everything that enters the brain and prevents the in-flow of viruses, bacteria and various undesirable or unnecessary materials.

The B.B.B. was discovered at the end of the 19th century by the German bacteriologist Paul Ehrlich who won a Nobel Prize in Medicine and Physiology in 1908 for his many contributions to Microbiology and Medicine. Dr. Ehrlich found that when he injected various dyes into animals, the dyes disseminated throughout the blood and stained all their tissues, except for the brain which remained unstained. Ehrlich wrongly hypothesized that the brain possesses low affinity for the injected dyes. One of

Ehrlich's students performed the other half of the experiment: he injected the dyes into the brain and found that only brain tissues were stained and not any body tissues. He, rightly, came to the conclusion that the dye, because of some barrier, could not enter from the brain to the body and vice versa.

The whole body, including the brain, is fed by a network of arteries out of which branch thinner and thinner blood arterioles and blood capillaries. The walls of blood capillaries are made of a single layer of endothelial cells that touch each other like tiles on a roof. In the connecting spaces between the endothelial cells of the capillaries there are gaps called 'intersections', through which blood cells and nutrients can pass from the blood to the brain tissues and back. However, these intersections in the brain are blocked by net-like protein fibers which form the B.B.B. and prevent a free in-and-out flow of needless materials from the capillaries into brain tissues.

Unfortunately, among the materials that cannot enter into the brain, are important drugs for the treatment of various brain diseases, including tumors. In order to cross the B.B.B, drugs must possess a molecular weight that is smaller than 400 Daltons, and also to be hydrophobic (that is, to be **uncharged** electrically). Hydrophobic molecules (which can dissolve in fatty substances) can pass through the B.B.B. since the walls of all cells in the body (including brain cells and the blood capillaries of the B.B.B), are made of a double lipid layer and can allow the infiltration of hydrophobic molecules. Non-hydrophobic nutrients that are required for the maintenance of the brain's health, can still enter brain tissues through specific nutrient receptors studded in the membranes of all the brain's blood capillaries.

To allow non-hydrophobic, electrically charged drugs, to cross the B.B.B., scientists have developed several technics to "sneak" them through. The best and most used technic is the "camouflaging/ masking" technic that we are going to use—electrically-charged impassable-drugs such as our Serotonin drug can be bound to a fatty or hydrophobic (uncharged) carrier molecule and thus, they can "fool" the B.B.B. Or else, they can be cut to a size that is **smaller than 400 molecular weight.** We shall use the cutting avenue in our **camouflaging and truncating!** The attachment method of non-hydrophobic to hydrophobic molecules is called the "Trojan horse" method after the mythological gigantic wooden horse in Homer's "Odyssey" The besieging Greek soldiers hid in the wooden horse, and the rest of the army sailed away. The jubilant Trojans, thinking that they finally won, breached a large entrance through their defending walls and dragged the horse inside the city to serve as a monument to their victory. At night, the Greek soldiers sneaked out from the wooden horse and conquered the city.

CHAPTER 9

Debbie's love turmoil

JOHN MET LUCIA EVERY THURSDAY to discuss her progress in the second project of the lab, and to plan the experiments for the next week. When they finished one such meeting, John said: "Luce, tell me something—what is your opinion of Debbie? You two already had a good chance to get acquainted, didn't you?" Lucia understood the real reason behind John's question and said: "Debbie is still new to research, but I am quite sure that she will soon prove to be a very good scientist. If I may gossip a little, I know that she is not married (John knew that already from Debbie's Curriculum Vitae) and that she does not have a boyfriend at the moment, which is rather surprising for such a beautiful girl."

Leaving John's office, Lucia reflected: "Debbie is very sweet and Ben is also very nice. These new 'acquisitions' to the lab should add new vitality and motivation to our work. Thank god and John, that our common project of Serotonin will soon take me away from my current work that involves organic syntheses with strong chemicals that affect my Asthma. This effect, happens, in spite of my use of the chemical fume hood during syntheses, and my Ventolin inhaler.

As for Debbie, I am sure that she will be a suitable girlfriend for John, despite their age-difference. I shall try to act as a match-maker between them, because I believe that both are interested in each other. Debbie even asked me, blushingly, one day, if I know whether John is now in a relationship. I know that John feels that lecturers and thesis supervisors should not invite their students to dates. Therefore, it will be a slow job, requiring my utmost tact. My best approach would be to enlist Ben for this enterprise and I am sure that he will agree to join ranks with me."

True to her resolve, Lucia invited Ben to coffee in in the lab's kitchen. They conferred at some length and then both of them returned to the lab. Ben immediately went to his office and phoned Moira.

Later in the afternoon, Ben entered John's office and said: "John, I hope that you will not be cross with me for what I am about to say. I dare say it, because I believe that we are friends and not just colleagues: I think that Debbie has a "crush" on you! Whenever you speak with her, she blushes and later makes some silly mistakes at work. In my opinion, not only do I think that the girl in love with you, but I also think that you are too. I can feel an undercurrent of sexual attraction between you that is so thick that one can almost cut it with a knife! Do the right thing for both of you and ask her to a date! Moira wanted to try to fix you up with some of her eligible new friends at work, but here you have a better "find", right under your nose!"

John opened his eyes in wonder and said: "Are you sure Ben? I am, indeed, strongly attracted to her. But you may be mistaken about her feelings. Perhaps she blushes because she is simply in awe of her thesis-adviser? If I ask her out and she refuses, it will be difficult for both of us to go on working together. Alternatively, if she accepts, I may come under heavy criticism from my colleagues when they hear about it. Worse still, I am much older and, therefore, may be unsuitable for her."

"Nonsense," said Ben. "Lucia also agrees with me that Debbie is very interested in you and that you suit each other perfectly. She suggested, and I agreed decline that Moira and I will invite all the lab's people including Lucia's husband, Tony, to dinner at our place this coming Saturday. On Friday, Lucia will say that she and Tony, unexpectedly, have to baby-sit with their grandson and cannot come. This will give you a chance to meet Debbie under sociable circumstances. Debbie does not possess a car so that you can drive her to our home and ask her for a date when you bring her back to her apartment. If she refuses to go out with you, which I doubt, you can ask her to keep it quiet between you two, and that you promise her that her rejection of your invitation will not affect your mutual work-relations even one whit."

John sat completely overwhelmed and said: "Why, you sneaky matchmakers! A fine ploy you concocted behind my back! I think I will sack you both!" And then he said: "Please Ben, give me some time to think about it."

"No way", said Ben. "I spoke with Debbie a few minutes ago, and she had already accepted and knows that you are going to pick her up in your car to dinner. I don't want to let the current situation between you remain unresolved!" John sighed and accepted the inevitable, since his refusal may endanger the success of the project.

On Saturday John had a hair-cut, bought two bottles of expensive boutique California wine and drove in the evening to pick up Debbie. On the short drive to dinner, they barely had time to talk and besides, John was a little tongue-tied sitting in the car next to the dolled-up, beautiful Debbie. When they arrived at Ben's and Moira's place, both of them breathed a little easier since the energetic Moira chatted and drew them into the conversation. Dinner went well because of the tasty meal and excellent wine. After dinner John drove Debbie to her apartment and accompanied her to the door. For a second, he almost asked her to a date, but "chickened out" and just said "good-bye". All the way back to his apartment, he chastised himself for his cowardly behavior and already started to compose an apologetic response to Ben and Lucia in answer to their impending questions on Monday.

Debbie locked her door disappointedly and waited near the door hoping that John may still knock. Then she drank a glass of water, went to bed and thought:

"I was hoping that John will ask me to-night for a date. I have a feeling that he wanted to, but held back. I am beginning to think that I made a mistake coming to his lab... I chose to work with him hoping to make him love me and to spend the all my life with him. Until now I have always succeeded in charming whomever I wanted. But they were not venerable university professors ...

If my mute courting will not succeed, I shall try to transfer to another lab, but it will be very difficult. I feel alive only when I am near him...

Debbie shook her head sadly and fell asleep, dreaming of John.

While the chemical company that was chartered by the scientists worked on the production of the Serotonin, John continued to prepare his lectures for his new course and to teach in his present one. Once a week they all met so that Ben and Debbie could report on their progress,. After each report Debbie thought:

"Immersed in work, I manage to drive away all thoughts of John. But, whenever we sit in a meeting, I sense an attraction between us and feel miserable that it is not consummated. I understand that it is difficult for him to ask me to a date, being older and my thesis supervisor. But, if he won't make a move soon, I shall ask him to a "semi-date". I shall pretend that I don't ski and ask him instruct me, saying that I heard that he had once already instructed John. If he agrees, during the instruction I shall pretend to slip, and shall stumble into his arms for support. I hope that this will break the ice, or more correctly, the snow between us" Then the lovelorn girl sighed and went back to work.

Analyses of the Serotonin the Mass Spectrometer confirmed their identity and purity.

John showed the formula of Serotonin that he removed from the Internet to his group, and said:"

"We did not discuss yet how to prepare the derivatives. Well, let me describe the methods to you: we shall remove the Amino group (NH_2) with a commercially bought Deaminase enzyme and call the resulting derivative "truncated Serotonin". Next, we shall pour bromic acid (HBr) on the hydroxyl group (OH) of Serotonin and heat the mixture. This action will add a Bromine molecule to the hydroxyl group to create OHBr. This Serotonin shall be our "Camouflaged Serotonin"! Simple, isn't it?

John had all the reagents ready, and the group, under John's tutelage, prepared the derivatives.

The work for that day stopped (it was already late in the afternoon anyway). Since a very important milestone has been reached, John invited the group for Pizza and beer. He also invited all the lab's people, including Debbie and Ben's and Lucia's spouses for the coming Saturday night to a posh sea food restaurant in the Brigham circle section of Boston.

CHAPTER 10

Performance of the crucial experiment and Debbie finally succeeds in her wooing

ON APRIL 15ᵀᴴ, A VERY important date in the history of mankind, John and his colleagues started a crucial experiment designed to test the efficacy of the Serotonin and its derivatives in mice. Testing was to be performed by feeding Serotonin and its derivatives immersed in a sugar solution, with a pipette to the mouths of the depressive Rouén mice and then submitting them to the "tail suspension" test.

On the day before the experiment, John taught Ben and Debbie how to perform the test: how to tie Rouen depressed mice to inclined poles and to register the twitching time s of the hung mice with the sort of clock used by competing chess players.

Before the start of the test, John addressed his group haltingly: "I am about to say something that may astound you: I am a rational scientist, but ever since I have started doing research, I carry a rabbit's foot in my pocket, It is the left hind foot of a rabbit shot in a graveyard in the new moon. I bought this amulet in a Woodoo shop in New-Orleans many years ago. I don't know if the rabbit was indeed shot in a grave-yard as the shop proprietor claimed, nor if it "works", but the fact is that ever since buying the amulet, I have never had really failed in any scientific experiment that I performed. If you yourselves have any such "scientific" implements that might draw "good energies" into the lab, can you bring them to to-morrow's crucial experiment?"

John expected some heavy joshing at his expense, but to his relief none came. Moreover, Lucia said: "I never take off the crucifix that I wear" and John said: "I carry a silver horse-shoe in my key-ring against evil eye and interestingly, I first met Moira, my lovely Irish girl for the first time on the very same day that I bought it, so, there you are." Lastly Debbie said: "I wear a "Hamsa" necklace that was given to me by my grand-mother. Hamsa is a good luck amulet in the form of a hand-palm and stands for the five Pentateuch books in the Old Testament." Awkwardly John summarized their discussion by saying: "Fine, we are well equipped for to-morrow's experiment!"

On the day of the test, the scientists prepared 4 sets of 4 tubes (one set for each of the scientists) and each one had 4 small tubes with the Serotonin, and the 3 derivatives (including the double derivative. They also had 4 jars with the 4 dyes they were going to paint on the backs of the fed mice that will correspond to the Serotonin and derivatives that they were fed, and 4 sets of 4 pipettes. Each scientist also had his own table of twisting results times, from which the average times of each time-point were to be calculated (each of the scientists wanted to participate in the feeding).

To start the experiment, each scientist added 0.1 milliliter of the each of the four tested materials to the tubes with the 0.5 milliliter of sugar solutions. Serotonin or each of its various derivatives, as in the table below:

1.   0.1 milliliter Serotonin – brown back. Abbreviated to:Con.

2. 0.1 milliliter Camouflaged Serotonin. – Red back. Abbreviated to: Cam-,
3. 0.1 milliliter Truncated Serotonin. - Yellow back – . Abbreviated to Trun-
4. 0.1mililiter truncated and camouflaged) – blue back – Abbreviated to Trun +- Cam.

Lucia prepared mouse cages, each contained randomly chosen 4 male or female- Rouén mice. Each mouse was transferred after pipette-feeding and the painting of the back, to signify what material the mice received. - A derivative or untreated Serotonin.

Prior to feeding, the scientists tested the 0-hr. basal-twitching-times of the mice. This was going to serve as the control zero time. Each scientist wrote the o twitching result in his table.0

At the 0.5-hour, 1hr, 2hr and the 3hr time-points since feeding, the scientists wrote the twitching times in their tables. The average results obtained from the 0- and 0.5-, 2hr. and 3hr hour measurements of the same-time 4 mice were calculated and are presented in the following table:

Table 1: Measurement of the lengths of the twitching times

Material Injected to the rats	0 hr. before Start of feeding	0,5 hr. after Start of feeding	2 hr. after start of feeding	3hr. after start of feeding
Serotonin.	61	160	145	155
Cam- Serotonin,	65	370	387	402
Tran-Serotonin	59	345	376	380

Tran and Cam-. Serotonin	62	356	400	390

All the mice showed increases in their twitching times relative to the unfed mice (0 time). John said at 1 hr. after the start in a hoarse and trembling voices: "The results look promising. If they will hold and even slightly improve, I shall be able to say that our "magical scientific amulets" worked . . So far, so good. But before we start to celebrate, let us wait for additional testing times, since "a single cuckoo does not herald spring." It is perplexing, though, that even the Control Serotonin which was supposed to serve as a negative control, appears to work, although presenting only about half of the twitching results of the derivatives! In addition, in case you have not noticed, there is one additional good omen – depressed Rouén male mice are apathetic and only rarely mate with the females. But the mice treated with Derivatives and even with the control Serotonin - started at 1 hour after feeding to sniff the females and to copulate with them.

John's eyes started to shine with the excellent interim results.

The scientists looked at the results up to 2 hr and 3 hr with great satisfaction: The mice fed with normal Serotonin and its derivatives all showed an increase in their twitching times relative to the unfed mice (0 time).

The results at the final 3 hrs. caused the scientists to forget their usual reserve/. Their joy was boundless! – They cheered enthusiastically, as if at the sight of an especially pleasing "dunk" by a Celtics' Forward!

John happily started a round of hugging and cheek-kissing,

starting with Ben and Lucia. When he came to Debbie, he hesitated a little, but then he held her waist gingerly, planning to kiss her cheek. However, Debbie, grasping her chance, moved her face as if by mistake and their lips met! Automatically John's arms tightened around her and he kissed her ardently, waiting for a rebuke that did not come …. When they "came back for air", John and Debbie looked at each other lovingly. Debbie sighed happily and said: "John, dearest, what took you so long! I have waited so long for your kiss and have almost given up on you!"

John answered enthusiastically: "Debbie, my love, I could not believe that a lovely girl like you would ever consider loving an older, chubby person like me!" Suddenly they became aware of their surroundings and looked with embarrassment at Ben and Lucia who raised their thumbs in approval …

The scientists went to lunch, with John and Debbie arm in arm. They chatted happily throughout lunch, discussing the 2 momentous events (the crucial experiment and the formation of the new couple) that just happened, ignoring the eyes of all the guests who watched them with interest.

On coming back to the lab, the new lovers went to John's office. They kissed again passionately. Eventually, Debbie came out of the office with a light step and a flushed and happy face. Ben and Lucia tidied the lab, stealing a peek at Debbie's happy face and winking discreetly at each other.

The exultant scientists went home and the new happy couple, as soon as they closed the door of John's apartment behind them, clung together kissed eagerly, and hastily helped each other to remove their clothes. and with yearning sighs stumbled to bed, diving into a sea of love and fulfillment. All evening and night they celebrated their new love, intimately learning to know each other's body, biography and soul.

When John and Debbie finally rested, completely satiated, John told Debbie that he thinks that judging by the results of the unchanged **high** 1 to 3 hr. results, the pharmacokinetics [6] of the derivatives of Serotonin (at least in Mice, and hopefully also in Men) are very good., Apparently, they are only slowly eliminated from the body. John told Debbie that his prediction is that just a single administration of the drug to humans per day should suffice.

John continued:" Now. Debbie my love, let us consider how to proceed. For the immediate future we have to cross three main milestones:

Will the Serotonin and/or its derivatives, be addictive? This point will be first tested in mice.

the Serotonin and/or its derivatives work successfully also in humans? I am fairly confident that it will, since the biochemistries and physiologies of mice and men are similar, although not identical.

So, will the Serotonin and/or its derivatives be addictive in humans? It is known that persons who enjoy a "runners' high" when they jog or train in a fitness club find it difficult, though not impossible, to stop exercising."

The next morning John said: "Debbie my love, we have known each other for two months and for several hours only as lovers. Still, I would like to offer you to move in with me. Please think about my offer." Debbie looked adoringly at John and immediately agreed. Thus started a wonderful partnership between them in research,

---

[6]   Pharmacokinetics-Pharmacokinetics is the study of the absorption and distribution of an administered drug in the body.

love, marriage and the raising of their children which was destined to last for many years.

Author's note: Copies of the tables of the Serotonin and derivatives' efficacy experiment in Rouén mice can be found in several museums which had been established in major cities across the world. These museums were established to commemorate the excellent finding of John's group and the Nobels of John and Ben…

CHAPTER 11

Testing whether the drug is habit-forming

A FEW DAYS AFTER THE Serotonin's successful efficacy test in mice, John invited his group to a meeting and said: "Dear friends, our next and very important step will be to test whether the derivatives will induce addiction in mice after prolonged use.

Lohn said: "This is how we will run the experiment: we shall prepare two regular cages which will house depressed Rouén mice and will contain **regular** food pellets or pellets with a mixture of **derivatives**. The pellet with derivatives will contain a smelly chemical. The mice will live in these cages for four weeks in order to allow them to develop addiction to the derivatives

I shall ask University's machine shop to prepare for us a special "torture" cage according to my design: one half of the floor in the cage is a heat-resistant asbestos plate, whereas the other half is made of a stainless-steel heating plate, controlled by a thermostat. At the far end the wall, adjacent to the heating plate, I shall place a container with the **SMELLY derivatives**

At the end of a 4 weeks' "habituation" period we shall remove the drugged and plain water from the "addiction or plain cages in order to create a presumed desire for the derivatives. as well as thirst. Next, we shall transfer one habituated mouse or a non-habituated mouse at a time to the "torture" cage whose heating plate will be turned on to 60° degrees Centigrade. The habituated mouse will run from the harmless asbestos plate towards the derivative-containing trough at the far end of the cage. If the mouse had developed addiction, it will persevere and drink from the smelly derivative in-spite of the heat under its paws. If it is not addicted, it will run back to the asbestos plate and give up any effort to drink.

On the night before the addiction test, John lay awake in bed, with success and failure scenarios flashing back and forth in his mind. When he finally fell asleep, he dreamed of human-faced mice that poked their tongues at him in derision.

Next day, bleary-eyed and tense and surrounded by his colleagues, John picked up one mouse from the derivatives' habituated group and placed it in the "torture cage." The mouse quickly ran from the asbestos half to the smelly derivative's trough. Unfortunately for the scientists, they saw that the" derivative mouse" was addicted. It drank its fill, raising one paw and another as a man on the beach crossing a particularly hot patch of sand. After drinking its fill, the mouse ran back to the asbestos plate, lied on its back and licked its burned paws. The non-habituated mouse who was treated with the whole Serotonin ran to the water and immediately ran back to the asbestos part without drinking. It should be remembered that the Rouen mice presented similar behavior: The same scenario repeated itself with 2 additional mice. The merciful Debbie and Lucia picked the poor mice and spread analgesic ointment on their paws. The gloomy scientists stood still, knowing that the future of the project is now rather uncertain because it showed that the derivatives are habit-forming.

John said in an anguished voice: "Ah, I knew it, I knew it! Things went too smoothly until now – it was too good to be true!"

With considerably reduced hopes John started to test the habituated mice. In seconds the scientists' mood changed: the first Serotonin mouse ran "happily" towards the trough, stepped on the heating plate and immediately made a hasty retreat back to the "safe" asbestos plate. A few seconds later it tried again and immediately retreated, as before. It crouched on the asbestos half with "a disappointed face" (this is probably what the scientists would have identified if they had been able to read the body—and "face" language of mice).

With shaking hands John repeated the experiment with two additional mice, obtaining the same result. The level of happiness rose from one mouse test to the other! John grabbed Debbie and started to waltz, humming a tune and Ben did the same with Lucia. A scientist who passed by the door of the animal facility was attracted by the mirth causing John to mumble some lame excuse for their unusual behavior... When they finally calmed down, John said: "Dear colleagues, by sheer luck, it seems that the small sequence that we changed from the 2 ends of the Serotonin turns the 2 derivative Serotonins, to addiction!!! The slight inhibitory action that we detected in the efficacy experiment! The results are quite clear. From now on, whole Serotonin is our only boy, or girl, if you wish! And we shall call it from now on SOMA!!!

We have made splendid breakthroughs in a very short time and this deserves celebration. Therefore, if you, Ben and Lucia, do not have any prior obligations for the coming week-end, I would like to invite you and your spouses and my Debbie at my expense to a resort on the beachfront of Cape Cod. I have heard good reports about this resort from some colleague and wanted to try it for quite a while. I was told that aside from the usual resort attractions it has an excellent chef. Ben and Lucia and Debbie agreed and John immediately made reservations.

The scientists and their spouses and Debbie drove to the resort and as soon as all the couples settled in their rooms John called the scientists to a short meeting in the resort's pub. He said: "Dear colleagues, I dislike to mix pleasure with work. Still, I want to remind you that we still have some obstacles to pass: we don't know yet if humans will also respond favorably to Serotonin like mice. If they are like mice, will they become addicted?

Then John added: "I don't want to discuss work on this weekend. But I just want quickly to say that on our immediate agenda will be the performance of pre-clinical drug-safety tests in various animals such as mice, dogs and monkeys. This is essential before FDA will let us test our Soma in humans. For this purpose, we shall hire the services of a company that specializes in this type of testing and had obtained a certification from FDA. This testing will take about two to three months. Let us cross our fingers and hope for good results from the company.

Now, I would like to make an announcement: if we shall succeed in our project, Harvard will get a large share of any profits accrued by selling the right to market Soma to a pharmaceutical or biotechnological company. Part of the profits come to me. Although I am the chief scientist and the holder of the Soma patent, I would like to share these profits equally between the four of us." This very generous offer by John rendered the other three scientists completely speechless. They immediately thanked him enthusiastically, but John waved aside their thanks saying that they deserved it!

Then Ben "piped": "Hey, Hey, hold it; this is not fair – Lucia and

I will get only one quarter each, while you and Debbie after you get married, will have two quarters!" After Ben dropped his "bomb", John stole a glance at Debbie who blushed. But Ben quickly said: "Hey, hey, I was kidding, I was kidding. I simply tried to promote for you the level of your relationship!" ...

The scientists set a time for dinner and Ben and Lucia hurried back to their rooms to relate the important news to their spouses.

Lucia related the news to Tony, her husband, and said: "what a generous boss I have. He could have kept all the profits from the Soma, the drug that we developed to himself. Instead, he decided to share it equally with us. If the Soma will succeed as an anti-depressant, it will greatly improve our financial situation."

Tony rejoiced too, but being a practical person, said: "Luce, let us wait until the Soma is certified before we go to the bank to cash on its success. Meanwhile, try to see if you could gently convince John to anchor his promise in a legal contract? ..."

Ben told Moira what happened in the meeting and she said happily: "Why, this is certainly in line with what I already know about John. If the drug would work, we would be able carry out our plans to have children earlier than we thought!"

CHAPTER 12

The writing of an IND and testing drug efficiency in elderly major depressed patients and anorectic girls

AFTER THE FINISH OF THE stability studies, John said: "The die is cast! Or, being a Latin scholar, I might say "Aleah Aica Est!" (the die is cast) ... Now the time has come to test the Serotonin on patients. Sometime ago I have told you that I shall be busy writing an IND application. A month ago, I finished writing it and immediately submitted it to FDA. FDA has one month to study any application, to deny it, to accept it, or to demand more data. If they did not say anything, it means that they are granting permission to start human clinical trials. The 30th day came and passed yesterday without any contesting letter from FDA! I did not want to bother you with this matter until now, but I can tell you that yesterday a huge burden came off my chest.

As I have already told you, we shall conduct limited scale clinical trials in patients. We already know from our own trial as volunteers that the Soma can cause happiness, euphoria and serenity and now we shall test whether it can also cure various mental disorders. For this, we shall choose suitable hospital wards or institutions and will ask their directors to perform such clinical trials with us. Most institutions and physicians are very interested in performing clinical trials since they will get financial support for their own research projects from the sponsors of the drug and can also publish papers on the outcome of the clinical trial, if it is successful.

The patients who will agree to take part in any trial (or their family if they are not mentally competent) will have to sign an "informed consent form" before the start. This form is a legally-defined form which lists for the patients all the key facts involved in the clinical trial. It includes trial details such as its purpose, duration, required trial procedures, risks and potential benefits. The "Informed consent form" is not a binding contract, since the patients can withdraw from the trial at any moment without penalty. The patients are also told that half of them (chosen at random) will receive the tested drug and the other half will receive a placebo. In case of a successful drug, the placebo-treated patients will also receive the drug at the end of the trial, free of charge."

When John finished his discourse, Debbie said: "John, when I had taken a statistics course, I was told that any survey, and in our case a clinical trial, should take into account as many variables as possible such as gender, race, age, type of population, economic status and so on. How is this going to be reflected in our upcoming clinical trials?"

John said: "Dear Debbie, you have raised a very pertinent and important question! Some years ago, I read an interesting study by several scientists whose names escape me now. They reviewed the best available clinical studies of psychiatric drugs for Depression, Bipolar Disorder, Schizophrenia and Attention Deficit Disorder that had involved something like 10,000 patients over several years, they found that not even one Native American was included in the studies and that only two or three of the patients were Hispanic.

Of about 3000 schizophrenia patients tested, only three were Asian. Also, among about 1000 patients with bipolar disorder (manic depressive disorder) there were no Hispanics or Asians. Blacks were better represented, but even their numbers in any one study were too small to tell the clinicians anything meaningful. Scientists have generally played down the role of cultural, ethnic and racial factors in the diagnosis, treatment and outcome of mental disorders. This is because modern psychiatry is based on the idea that mental illnesses are primarily organic disorders of the brain. This approach suggests that the symptoms, course, and treatment of disorders ought to be the same whether the patients are from the Caribbean, Canada or Cambodia.

Major mental disorders like Schizophrenia, Bipolar Disorder, Depression, etc. are found worldwide across all racial and ethnic groups. Based on available evidence, the prevalence of mental disorders for racial and ethnic minorities in the United States is similar to that for whites. Therefore, my dear Debbie, and also because of the small number of the patients that we shall study in each trial, by necessity we shall ignore the effects of gender, age, ethnicity and economic status."

John decided that the first limited clinical trial that they will perform will be carried out with Anorexia nervosa patients and said: "As you know, Anorexia nervosa is an extremely serious eating disorder expressed by a paralyzing fear of getting fat. The patients, mostly ten to eighteen years old girls, live under a regimen of self-imposed starvation in order to lose weight. In more advanced stages of the disorder the patients may even feel a loathing of food and cannot eat even if they wanted to. This disorder causes terrible results—the extreme fasting causes a complete disruption and destruction of all body systems. The body temperature declines, the pulse slows down and the body's resistance against infection disappears. Finally, very serious heart problems develop that cause death. About 5% of all anorectic patients die within several years.

Researchers believe that the reasons for anorexia nervosa are a combination of psychological, biological and socio-cultural pressures at the start of puberty: according to a psychoanalytical approach, the patients (most of them are girls) do not want to mature and therefore fast in order to postpone as much as possible their sexual maturation (indeed, their breasts do not develop and their menstruation cycle either does not appear at all, or disappears). According to other theories, the disorder is due to problematic family ties, especially with the mothers. The girls feel that the only way left to them for independence and control of their fates and bodies is self-starvation.

Other theories stress the importance of peer pressure: the need to be thin and beautiful. Ever since the successful model Twiggy, girls today, even very young ones, still believe that they need to be super-skinny in order to be sexy.

There is also a genetic approach to unraveling the cause of anorexia. Geneticists believe that anorectics are prey to a genetic pre-disposition to various emotional disorders such as distress, self-hatred, anxiety and depression. Studies have showed that 40% of all anorectics suffer from medium to major depression. It is this finding that prompted me to try our Soma on anorectics."

All of John's group expressed their approval for the performance of the proposed study and Debbie also said that she met a couple of anorectic girls in the past and agreed that were in a sorry mess.

In order to perform the trial, John approached one of his

colleagues, Professor Enid LeBlanc, who was the director of the psychiatric ward in the Massachusetts General Hospital in Boston and also lectured on clinical psychology at Harvard's Medical and graduate schools.

John described the group's personal experiences as volunteer users of the Soma to Professor LeBlanc and also said that they have received an IND approval from FDA to perform human trials. Professor LeBlanc will agree to carry out a clinical trial with the anorectic patients in her psychiatric ward. She also said that she had waited long for a suitable drug for the treatment of this affliction, adding that the anorectics, at present, take SSRI drugs (mainly Prozac) but with only indifferent results.

Professor LeBlanc recruited 16 anorectic girls by promising them that throughout the 6-week trial they will not be fed forcefully either by a feeding tube or by infusion to the vein. But she also told them that they will have to attend all meals and that their eating be supervised by the nurses, as before. The study was a double blind one: only John and his group knew what each coded inhaler contained. The ward's nurses supervised the daily inhalation process and the trial patients were weighed once a week and their mental state was also evaluated once a week by a questionnaire called the Beck Depression Inventory (BDI) in order to test if there was any improvement in their depressive state. The BDI questionnaire, developed by Dr. Aaron T. Beck, is used to evaluate of the depressive status, since there are no chemical blood tests for determining the severity of depression. The BDI is A 21-question, multiple-choice, self-report inventory that is filled by the patients themselves, is designed for individuals aged 13 and over and is composed of items relating to symptoms of depression such as hopelessness and irritability, cognitions such as guilt, or feelings of being punished, physical symptoms such as fatigue, weight gain or loss and interest in sex. When the test is scored, a value of 0 to 3 is assigned for each answer and the total score obtained assesses the existence and severity of the depression. The standard cut-offs in the BDI are as follows: A score of 0-13: minimal depression; 14–19: mild depression; 20–28: moderate depression, and 29–63: severe depression.

John said: "Dear colleagues, since the BDI is pivotal to our future work, let us take the test ourselves. I shall bet that our scores will be very low. Just note that the questions in sections 16 and 18 ("Changes in Sleeping Pattern" and "Changes in Appetite") should produce only one score." John distributed copies of the inventory that Enid gave him and he and his group filled them. True to his prediction, all of them had a very low score.

Beck Depression Inventory (BDI, for self-administration):

Symptom	depression symptom	Self-Grading
1. Sadness	0 I do not feel sad	
	1 feel sad much of the time	
	2 I am sad all the time	————
	3 I am so sad or unhappy that I cannot stand it	
2. Pessimism	0 I am not discouraged about my future	
	1 I feel more discouraged about my future than I used to be	
	2 I do not expect things to work for me	————
	3 I feel my future is helpless and it will only get worse	

3. Past Failure	0 I do not feel like a failure	
	1. I have failed more than I should have	
	2 As I look back, I see a lot of failures	
	3 I feel I am a total failure as a person	
	2. I don't get as much pleasure as I used before	
	1 I don't enjoy things as much as I used to	
	2 I get very little pleasure from the things I used to enjoy	
	3 I can't get any pleasure from the things I used to enjoy	
5. Guilty Feeling	0 I don't feel particularly guilty	
	1 I feel guilty over many things that I have done or should have done	
	2 I feel quite guilty most of the time	
	3 I feel guilty all the time	
6. Punishment Feeling	0 I don't feel I am being punished	
	1 I feel that I may be punished	
	2 I expect to be punished	
	3 I feel I am being punished	
7. Self-Dislike	0 I feel the same about myself as ever	
	1 I have lost confidence in myself	
	2 I am disappointed in myself	
	3 I dislike myself	
8. Self Criticalness	0 I don't criticize or blame myself more than usual	
	1 I am more critical of myself than I used to be	
	2 I criticize myself for all my faults	
	3 I blame myself for everything bad that happened	

9. Suicidal thoughts or wishes	0 I don't have any thoughts of killing myself	
	1 I have thoughts of killing myself. But I would not carry them out	
	2 I would like to kill myself	
	3 I would kill myself if I had a chance	
10. Crying	3 I would kill myself if I had a chance	
	0 I don't cry any more than I used to	
	1 I cry more than I used to	
	2 I cry over every little thing	
	3 I feel like crying, but I can't	
11. Agitation	0 I am no more restless or wound-up than usual	
	1 I feel more restless or wound-up than usual	
	2 I am so restless and agitated that it is hard to stay still	
	3 I am so restless or agitated that I have to keep moving or doing something	
12. Loss of Interest	0 I have not lost interest in other people or activities	
	1 I am less interested in other people or things than before	
	2 I have lost most of my interests in other people or things	
	3 It is hard to get interested in anything	
13. Indecisiveness	0 I make decisions about as well as ever	
	1 I find it more difficult to make decisions than usual	
	2 I have much greater difficulty in making decisions than I used to	
	3 I have trouble making any decisions	

14. Worthlessness	0 I do not feel I am worthless	
	1 I do not consider myself as worthwhile and useful as I used to	
	2 I feel more worthless as compared to other people	
	3 I feel utterly worthless	
15. Loss of Energy	0 I have as much energy as ever	
	1 I have less energy than I used to have	
	2 I don't have enough energy to do very much	
	3 I don't have enough energy to do anything	
16. Changes in Sleeping Pattern	0 I have not experienced any change in my sleeping pattern	
	1a I sleep somewhat more than usual	
	1b I sleep somewhat less than usual	
	2a I sleep a lot more than usual	
	2b I sleep a lot less than usual	
	2a I sleep a lot more than usual	
	2b I sleep a lot less than usual	
	3a I sleep most of the day	
	3b I wake up 1-2 hours early and can't go back to sleep	
17. Irritability	0 I am no more irritable than usual	
	1 I am more irritable than usual	
	2 I am much more irritable than usual	
	3 I am irritable all the time	

18. Changes in Appetite	0 I have not experienced any change in my appetite	
	1a My appetite is somewhat less than usual	
	1b My appetite is somewhat greater than usual	
	2a My appetite is much less than before	
	2b My appetite is much greater than usual	
	3a I have no appetite at all	
	3b I crave food all the time	

The experiment with the anorectic girls started and their end-of-weeks' weights and Beck's scores were recorded. The weight-increases and the BDI results that were obtained by the end of the clinical trial relative to the start, were summarized in a table:

Summary of the results of the 6-week trial in anorectic girls

patient No.	Increase in weight (kg)	Change in Beck's Score*
1	2.9	+3
2	7.9	-15
3	8.7	-22
4	2.1	+3
5	8.0	-25
6	2.1	+4
7	8.4	-25
8	2.2	+3

9	9.0	-22
10	8.5	-14
11	2.6	+4
12	1.2	+3
13	7.6	-20
14	2.4	+5
15	7.7	-15
16	2.0	+5

*) Note: A minus sign in the Beck's score means a reduction in the degree of depression

After the opening of the code, the mean results were calculated for the 8 SOMA and the 8 Placebo patients. These mean results are presented in the next table:

**Means of weight-gains and change in Beck's scores
for the SOMA and the Placebo patients**

Type of treatment	mean change in weight (Kg)	Mean change in Beck's score
	+8.2	-19.7
Placebo	+2.2	+3.8

The results of the tables indicated very clearly that the Serotonin patients exhibited great improvements in mood and nice increases in weights. The joyful parents of the improved girls clamored to know the identity of their benefactors, made visits to the lab, and inundated the group with flowers and chocolates. Learning from this experience, the group decided to demand anonymity from the staffs that will perform their clinical trials in the future.

At John's request, Professor LeBlanc prepared a detailed report of the results which was to be presented eventually to pharmaceutical companies. She also wrote a scientific paper on the results which also bore the four scientists' names, but she was forced to wait for John's green light for its submission to a journal.

Professor LeBlanc asked the group for additional inhalers for all her other anorectic patients, but John was forced to refuse saying that by FDA laws he is unable to fulfil her wish. On hearing his answer, she sighed, knowing that she has to continue to try to save the lives of her anorectic patients with conventional feeding methods and with SSRIs. To "console" her John said: "dear Enid, I was very happy with your excellent handling of our trial and I plan to carry additional clinical trials with you for more disorders if you would agree." And being in an expansive and elated mood because of their success in their first trial, he recited the memorable lines of the poem that was written by Emma Lazarus in 1883 and is inscribed inside the Statue of Liberty:

"Give me your tired, your poor, your huddled masses yearning to breathe free, the wretched refuse of your teeming shore.

Send these, the homeless, tempest-tossed to me,

I lift my lamp beside the golden door!"

Both Enid and John smiled, shook hands on their "contract" and went their ways.

In the aftermath of the successful clinical trial with the elderly frail persons, John decided to perform a clinical trial with patients of Major Depressive Disorder. John considered this target to be the most appropriate one for the Serotonin and Ben, remembering his depressed friend from Philadelphia, as well as Debbie and Lucia, whole-heartedly agreed with him.

John said: "after the successful culmination of the anorexia trial I promised Enid that we would perform additional clinical trials with her. Two weeks ago, I called her and suggested a trial with her major depression patients. Let me tell you that her shout of joy on the phone caused me to lose the hearing in my right ear for a few seconds…As a result, she had been recruiting, and told me yesterday that all her major depression patients from the outpatient clinic agreed to participate in the trial.

When we go to meet Enid, I already want you to know some facts about this very serious affliction and its presumed causes. Ben is already familiar with the subject, but you, my lovely Debbie and my faithful Lucia, hark to my discourse:

"The words of Stephen Foster in his song "Old folks at home" ("Way down Upon the Swanee River") quite aptly describe the state of many depressive patients:

"All de world am sad and dreary, Ebry where I roam. . ."

Major depressive disorder, also known as recurrent depressive disorder, clinical depression, major depression, unipolar depression, or unipolar disorder, is a mental disorder characterized by an all-encompassing low mood accompanied by low self-esteem, and by a loss of interest or pleasure in normally enjoyable activities. It is an extremely debilitating condition which adversely affects a person's family, his work or school life, sleeping and eating habits and general health. Depressed people may be preoccupied with, or ruminate over, thoughts and feelings of worthlessness, inappropriate guilt or regret, helplessness, hopelessness and self-hatred. In severe cases, depressed people may have symptoms of psychosis which include delusions or, less commonly, unpleasant hallucinations. Other symptoms of depression include poor concentration and memory, withdrawal from social situations and activities, reduced sex drive and thoughts of death or suicide. Insomnia is also common, and the patients have shorter life expectancies than those without depression, in part because of greater susceptibility to physical illnesses and suicide. About 3.4% of people with major depression in the United States commit suicide, or, put another way—up to 60% of people who committed suicide had major depression or another mood disorder.

The most common onset time of major depression is between the ages of 20 and 30 years, with a later peak between 30 and 40 years. Diagnosis is based on the patient's self-reported experiences, his behavior as described by relatives or friends, and a mental status examination such as the Beck Depression Inventory.

Typically, patients are treated with tricyclic antidepressants and anti-psychotic drugs and in many cases also receive psychotherapy. Hospitalization may be necessary in cases with associated self-neglect or a significant risk of harm to self or others.

A minority of major depression cases are treated with electroconvulsive therapy (ECT) under general anesthesia. Most recently, major depression is also treated by a technique known as Repetitive transcranial magnetic stimulation (rTMS) in which a powerful magnetic field is used to stimulate the brain. This therapy does not require anesthesia as with ECT and does not cause any confusion or memory loss such as those encountered with ECT. Both rTMS and ECT treatments are efficient, but require up 20 sessions to obtain good results and therefore cannot be used widely as, hopefully, our Serotonin."

Forearmed with the information concerning major depression that John fed them, the scientists met Enid who told them that she recruited 72 ambulatory patients that make regular weekly visits to her out-patient clinic. The trial was again a double blind one. The patients were distributed into 2 groups with about an equal distribution of ages and gender. The trial was slated to last for 4 weeks. The placebo inhaler patients received their regular drugs, while the SOMA inhaler patients were given placebo pills that looked and tasted just like their previous regular drugs. They were asked to report every week to the out-patient clinic and to describe their mental condition.

One week after the start of the trial, Enid called John and his group and happily informed them that about half of the patients reported a feeling of great serenity and happiness which was also reflected in their faces. Instead of looking ashen and miserable, their lines of misery completely disappeared. The opening of the code at the end of the four-week trial completely vindicated Enid's empirical observations.

John told his group that he plans to offer the major depression indication as the one which be tested in future big clinical trials intended to obtain certification by the FDA.

CHAPTER 13

The break into the lab, the stealing of the drugs. Ben solves a big quandary. the testing of the drug in schizophrenia, bipolar depression, DID, PTSD, and drug addiction

A FEW DAYS AFTER THE completion of the trial with the elderly frail and major depression patients, John and Debbie came early to the lab and saw that its normally locked door was ajar. On entering they saw that the lab was in complete mess: bottles with chemicals lay broken, the refrigerators and freezers were open and glass tubes and containers lay broken on the floor. The two big safes that John bought for storage of the inhalers remained closed, but bore the signs of break-in efforts. John called the campus police who questioned the building's security guards. Investigation revealed that a man wearing work coveralls and carrying a toolbox entered last evening saying that he was called for an emergency repair of an instrument in Professor Novick's lab. Since the man knew John's name, the guard, new to the job, let him in without asking for credentials. This "technician" left after 10 PM. John came to the obvious conclusion that one of the anorectic girls of the trial or her parents, told their friends about the new "wonder drug" and the names of the scientists who invented it... John immediately asked the campus maintenance unit to install a strong break-safe door at the entrance to the lab at his grant's expense, and to put steel grilles on the windows.

The whole group worked hard all day to put the lab back in order and to obtain new chemicals and materials to replace the spilled ones. Tired after their hard work, John and Debbie went to bed. John, who suffered occasionally from insomnia, went over the day's events and finally was ready to "count sheep." Suddenly he sat in bed, grabbed his head and moaned softly, in order not to wake Debbie.

"Woe is me! He thought. "What shall we do? We have created a monster – an extremely dangerous drug that is worse than all street drugs combined! We shall never be able to market it. Within a short time, news of the non-addictive euphoria-inducing-drug will spread all over the world. As a result, all the producing plants and all the drug-stores will be plundered by criminals for selling in the streets. Even the biggest imaginable pharmaceutical factories in the world not be able to produce enough inhalers to satisfy the needs of the billions of inhabitants of the world. This will lead to the eruption of drug wars world-wide!

Thus, John lay awake all night in agony. He decided not to wake Debbie in order to save her a few hours of sorrow.

Next day, John came bleary-eyed and withered to the lab. Debbie already saw his state early morning and pressed him to tell her what was wrong. In an anguished voice he told her of his gloomy prediction and she sadly agreed that he was right, but gamely tried to console him. When Ben and Lucia arrived, John told them of his fears and apprehensions. They sobered up when he described the scenario as he envisioned it last night, and sadly admitted that he was right.

At the end of the gloomy discussion, Ben went to his office, planning to call Moira and to tell her of the unfortunate ruin of the 's prospects. suddenly he froze in his chair and started to mull over a glimmer of an idea which became more and more coherent with each passing second! He was sure that his idea could save the drug for the world! He hurried to John's office and said: "John, Eureka! I have a tremendous idea that will save our brain-child."

John raised his crestfallen face and extinguished eyes to Ben who said: "Listen my friend! There are several philanthropic billionaires in the US and the world who regularly contribute a part of their fortune to welfare through foundations that they had established, and their number is steadily growing. Among them are the "heavy" and well-known billionaires Bill Kelly and Warren Brooks. Bill Kelly established the Bill and Jeanne Kelly foundation to which both Kelly and Brooks contributed very large sums of money. The foundation's aim is to increase healthcare and education and help poor people in the world. We shall approach Kelly and Brooks first, describe our results, show them Professor LeBlanc's and Dr. Benchley's summary reports and the IND granting by the FDA. In addition, we shall let them try the soma for themselves so that they will understand how important it is going to be for all humanity. I am quite sure that we can persuade them, or some other philanthropic billionaires, to help us certify the drug and to build huge factories all over the world in order to produce secretly billions of soma inhalers. Only after we would accumulate the necessary large number of inhalers for all humanity several times over, we shall publicize our invention and distribute the Soma all humanity, free of charge!"

John opened his eyes in wonder and the color came back to his face. He stood up, hugged Ben and they went happily together to the lab. John, pointing to Ben, said: "Look at this guy and praise him among all nations and extol his virtues for all to hear! He is the MAN, our hero! He found an excellent way to save our soma!" Ben then described his ideas to the girls, who applauded him enthusiastically.

Debbie said: "What a great idea, I am sure that it will work. But, in the meantime, how can we block leaks about the drug from the participants of our future clinical trials?"

Riding on the wave of the creative imagination that he had already displayed, Ben said: "First, we shall ask the medical staffs of our next trials not to divulge our identity. Secondly, the medical staffs will warn all the tested patients that the drug will only work on them alone, since it will correct a defective gene that they carry and that caused their disorder. They will also tell the patients not share their inhalers with family or friends, because healthy people lack the defective gene and, as a result, even one whiff of the drug will damage their brains! The patients will be told also that they will receive one inhaler with 31 daily doses per month and that if they share their inhalers with family or friends, they will miss doses at the end of the month, and will suffer very painful withdrawal symptoms."

The rest of the day went on joyfully since the scientists knew that they had averted an unforeseen huge disaster and that, thanks to John's and Ben's acumen, they had just barely missed setting the world on fire!

John said: "As I have already told you in the past, each new drug must undergo rigorous clinical testing in many patients before it is approved by health authorities. The performance of such testing requires a great deal of effort and large sums of money. Therefore, in addition to the hiring of a company for the large-scale production of soma inhalers for us, we shall ask Kelly and Brooks (or any other philanthropists that will agree to help) to contract the services of a large CRO company. Such a company specializes in the performance of clinical trials for sponsors of new drugs. It recruits patients, medical centers, physicians, nurses and pharmacists, maintains a medical file for each patient, performs the statistical analyses of the results of the trials and prepares the extensive paperwork required by FDA prior for the approval of a drug. Meanwhile, we shall continue our limited clinical trials in order to determine which additional disorders the soma can, hopefully, cure.

"Dear friends, we have been marvelously successful with our soma till now, obtaining a 1.000 batting average.

These summaries described how the soma so successfully cured their patients. The clinicians also wrote that they regularly take the soma themselves and how happy and serene they are as a result.

Following their success in the clinical trials with the anorectic patients, the elderly frail persons and the major depression patients, the scientists started a clinical trial with schizophrenic patients. True to John's promise to Professor Leblanc, the trial was to be carried out again at her outpatient clinic. Before planning the trial, John and his group turned to the Internet sites of the National Institute of Mental Health in order to learn more about the disorder. This is what they read:

"Schizophrenia is a mental disorder typified by disintegration of the process of thinking and of emotional responsiveness. It is most commonly manifested by auditory hallucinations, paranoid or bizarre delusions, disorganized thinking and is accompanied by significant social or occupational dysfunctions. The onset of symptoms typically occurs in young adulthood, with a global lifetime prevalence of around 1.5%. Diagnosis is based on the patient's self-reported experiences and observed behavior.

The development of Schizophrenia in patients is ascribed to 3 factors:

1. A pathologic factor – a problem in the development of the embryo's brain, or degeneration of the brain's neurons after their development.

2. A genetic factor – when one of the parents is schizophrenic, the frequency of schizophrenia in his offspring goes up to 10% and when both parents have schizophrenia, the frequency of the disorder goes up to 40%. When one sibling of identical twins is sick, the other one has a 50% chance of becoming schizophrenic. Still, schizophrenia is, apparently, not linearly inherited; otherwise, the occurrence in both siblings should have been 100%.

3. Schizophrenics have an overactive dopamine system that acts in the mesolimbic pathway of the brain. Therefore, Dopamine antagonists can help regulate this system by "turning down" Dopamine activity and are helpful in some of the patients.

Despite the etymology of the term—from the Greek roots: skhizein "to split" and phrēn "mind"—schizophrenia is not a "split mind" disorder. The "real" split mind disorder is called" dissociative identity disorder (DID)", which is also known as "multiple personality disorder" or "split personality." People often mistakenly confuse schizophrenia with DID.

In more serious cases of schizophrenia—where there is risk to the patient himself and to others—involuntary hospitalization may be necessary. Schizophrenia is thought, mainly, to affect cognition, but it also contributes to chronic problems with emotion and behavior, major depression and anxiety disorders. The lifetime occurrence of drug abuse in schizophrenic patients is around 40%. Social problems such as long-term unemployment and poverty are common. As a result, the prevalence of Schizophrenia is very high among untreated homeless people—around 10-20%. The average life expectancy of people with this disorder is 10 to 12 years shorter than of those without it, due to increased prevalence of physical health problems and a high suicide rate (about 5%).

As already described above, schizophrenic patients may experience hallucinations (most commonly hearing voices), delusions (often bizarre or persecutory in nature) and disorganized thinking and speech. The latter may range from a loss of train of thought, to sentences that are only loosely connected in meaning, up to an incoherent speech known as" word salad." There is often an observable pattern of emotional difficulty, such as lack of responsiveness or motivation. As a result of impairment in social cognition, the patients exhibit symptoms of paranoia and social isolation. In one subtype, the person may be largely mute, remain motionless in bizarre postures, or exhibit purposeless agitation. The peak years for the onset of schizophrenia are late adolescence and early adulthood.

Schizophrenia is described in terms of positive and negative (or deficit) symptoms. The term positive symptoms refer to symptoms that are present in schizophrenics and not in healthy people. These include delusions, auditory hallucinations and thought disorders. Negative symptoms refer to behaviors exhibited by healthy persons, but are absent in schizophrenic ones. Common positive symptoms include flat or blunted emotions, poverty of speech, inability to experience pleasure, lack of desire to form relationships and lack of motivation. Research suggests that negative symptoms contribute more to poor quality of life, functional disability and the burden on others, than do positive ones.

Several years ago, the plight of schizophrenic patients came to the attention of the general public in a touching movie "A Beautiful Mind "that described the life of John Forbes Nash who won the Nobel Prize in Economic

Sciences in 1994.

As already described above, schizophrenics exhibit unusually high dopamine activity in the mesolimbic pathway of the brain. The mainstay of treatments of schizophrenia are antipsychotic drugs such as Clozapine, Risperdal or Zyprexa. These drugs block Dopamine receptors, prevent their activity and can induce complete recovery in up to 20% of the patients, whilst in others they are only partially effective. However, the side-effects of these anti-psychotic drugs are very significant: inability to start moving, or inability to stand still, involuntary spasm in the face, throat, eyes, tongue or chin, marked increase in weight and loss of libido. As a result, many patients refuse to take them. Recently, however, anti-schizophrenia drugs such as Risperdal and others are administered as depot medications by injection. These drug depots allow a slow release of drug throughout 2-4 weeks and cause lighter side-effects. At present, however, these depot drugs are very expensive.

Schizophrenia is a terrible affliction for life, and Enid and John's group hoped to cure the patients, or at least to alleviate their symptoms without the bad side-effects encountered with antipsychotic drugs. Their hope for cure or improvement was based on John's finding of the new "Cipramil to Serotonin pathway". Since Cipramil decreases the synthesis of Dopamine and increases that of Serotonin, they hoped that the soma will have a good chance of helping the schizophrenics and the Serotonin that is free from side effects will work even much better!

As in all the group's clinical trials till now, the trial with the schizophrenic patients was a double-blind one. It included 64 men and women of which half of them received Serotonin free of side effects inhalers plus a placebo pill that looked exactly like their usual anti-psychotic drug, while the other half received placebo inhalers and their previous regular drug.

Success in the trial was immediately apparent and unequivocal. The condition of about half of the patients improved markedly after 2-4 days from the start of the trial, regardless of whether they suffered from positive or negative symptoms. Therefore, the double-blind code was eagerly broken much earlier than planned and confirmed that the marvelously cured patients were indeed those treated with Serotonin free-of-side-effects inhalers.

As a result of their victory over one of the worst mental disorders, John decided to offer the schizophrenia indication for testing by "their" future CRO company (in addition to the Major Depression indication).

Year 2013

After the successful termination of the schizophrenia trial,

John addressed his group: "Dear colleagues, so far, we have been very successful in proving the efficacy of soma in several mental disorders; but, "eating whets the appetite." Therefore, with a certain degree of justified Hubris, I am greedy for more successes. Before, as an experimental neuropharmacologist and a teacher, I knew a lot about mental disorders in theoretical terms but I was mostly interested in fighting depression. But now, when confronted face to face with the poor patients that we encountered in Enid's psychiatric ward, I am keen to cure all mental disorders, no less"... John's Colleagues nodded their heads in agreement.

John and his group met Enid and her staff again and she said: "Dear marvelous colleagues, you have come to us like Manna from heaven and like spring water in the desert! Before you came, my staff and I stumbled along sadly with only middling success. Now, all that has changed! Therefore, I hope that God and the soma, will let us cure Bi-polar disorder. This disorder, which as you well know. is also known as manic-depressive disorder, is a very serious mental illness that causes sudden shifts in a person's mood, energy and ability to function. The disorder was termed "Bipolar", because its patients shift from a pole of Mania—an overly joyful and overexcited state—to a pole of Depression and back again. These shifts in mood are quite different from the normal ups-and-downs that everyone encounters through life. The symptoms of bipolar disorder are extremely severe. Many famous leaders, musicians, writers and artists were identified as suffering from the disorder, either by their historically-documented behavior, or by their own public disclosures. Let me mention just a few of many names: Vincent Van-Gogh, Jackson Pollock, Theodore Roosevelt, Virginia Wolfe, Edgar Allen Poe, Abraham Lincoln, Johann Wolfgang von

Goethe, Napoleon Bonaparte, Charles Dickens, Winston Churchill, Robert Schumann, Ludwig van Beethoven, Jack London, Charles Dickens, William Faulkner, Ernest Hemingway, Mark Twain, Rosemary Clooney, Florence Nightingale, Lord Byron, Alfred Lord Tennyson, Hermann Hesse, John Keats, Sylvia Plath, Hans Christian Andersen, Vivian Leigh, Stephen Fry and Kurt Cobain. Of this very limited list alone three persons had committed suicide: Hemmingway, Plath and Cobain.

Then Enid added: "The symptoms of the manic episode of the disorder are as follows: In mania, the patients exhibit a long period of feeling "high"—an overly happy or outgoing mood, but they are also irritable, feeling agitated, "jumpy" or "wired-up." During this episode, the patients talk at a very fast rate, jump from one idea to another, their thoughts are constantly racing, they are easily distracted and start new projects without much thought. In addition, they need only little sleep and exhibit an unrealistic belief in their abilities. As a result, they take part in a lot of pleasurable high-risk behaviors such as spending sprees, impulsive sex and risky business investments.

Patients with bipolar disorder also experience episodes of hypomania. During hypomanic episodes, the patient may have increased energy and creativity levels but these are not as severe as in typical mania and do not require emergency care. Patient in a hypomanic episode feels very well, are highly productive and function well. They may not even feel that anything is wrong with them and only their family and friends can recognize their hypomanic symptoms. The hypomanic state does not last long and eventually converts into a manic or a depressive state.

Sometimes, a person with severe episodes of mania or depression may also experience psychotic symptoms such as hallucinations or delusions. As a result, such patients are sometimes wrongly diagnosed as having schizophrenia.

The symptoms of a depressive episode include the following: a long period of feeling worried or empty, a loss of all interest in activities once enjoyed (including sex), feeling tired or "slowed down", having problems concentrating, remembering and making decisions, being restless, sad or irritable, changing eating—sleeping—or other habits, thinking of death or suicide, or actually even attempting it.

Bipolar disorder is commonly treated with mood stabilizers such as Lithium and Valproic acid. Sometimes, antipsychotic—and antidepressant drugs are also used along with the mood stabilizer. In general, patients continue treatment with mood stabilizers for years. But, as is the case with schizophrenia, many patients stop taking their drugs because of their very serious side-effects:

1. Lithium's side-effects include loss of coordination, excessive thirst, frequent urination, blackouts, seizures, slurred speech, fast or slow or irregular or pounding heartbeat, hallucinations, changes in vision, itching, rash, swelling of the eyes, face, lips, tongue, throat, hands, feet, ankles, or lower part of the legs.

2. Valproic acid's side-effects are changes in weight, nausea, stomach pain, vomiting, anorexia and loss of appetite. This drug can also cause damage to the liver or the pancreas.

Some of the patients stop taking their drugs for fear that they will curtail the pleasure and flow of the creativity that they experience during the hypomanic stage. Therefore, dear saviors," "concluded Enid in a way that made us blush, "let us try to help these really miserable people."

Enid enrolled 78 outpatients that were in an active state of mania or depression at the time of the trial. As in the previous trials, one half of the patients, chosen at random, received soma inhalers and placebo pills that looked and tasted like their regular drugs and the other half received their regular true drug plus placebo inhalers.

The scientists entered the trial with some trepidation for 2 reasons:

A. Aside from the knowledge that bipolar disorder also has a genetic back-ground, the mechanism of its induction was still obscure.

B. The scientists were sure that the soma inhales, because of its already proven efficiency, will help patients in the depression pole, but they were afraid that the -inhalers might quickly cause them to switch from depression into a manic stage.

In spite of the group's misgivings, the soma inhalers worked beautifully! Even before opening the blind code, it became obvious that one half of the patients exhibited a complete cure! Enid and her staff were sure that they must belong to the soma group since they had never witnessed such miraculous cures before: patients in a manic episode moved from a manic to a hypomanic state in one day and within two additional days started to express the same serenity and bliss expected from a soma treatment. The depressive patients in this same half also became happy and serene after one or two days. At Enid's urgent behest and because of John's own impatience, the scientists hastily broke the double-blind code and were relieved and overjoyed to find that all the miraculous cures indeed happened in the soma group!

All the trial's patients, whether they were from the soma or Placebo groups received 'take home' soma inhalers for 12 months. They were instructed to report back to the clinic during this period in case of unexplained reversals or unusual bad side-effects. No patient reported back early. As usual, all of the patients were told to prevent their relatives or friends from trying the soma since it is extremely dangerous to "normal" people . . . -, let us try to cure Bi-polar disorder. This disorder, which is also known as manic-depressive disorder, is a very serious mental illness that causes sudden shifts in a person's mood, energy and ability to function. The disorder was termed "Bipolar", because its patients shift from a pole of Mania—an overly joyful and overexcited state—to a pole of depression and back again. These shifts in mood are quite different from the normal ups-and-downs that everyone encounters through life. The symptoms of bipolar disorder are extremely severe. Many famous leaders, musicians, writers and artists were identified as suffering from the disorder, either by their historically-documented behavior, or by their own public disclosures. Let me mention just a few of many names: Vincent Van-Gogh, Jackson Pollock, Theodore Roosevelt, Virginia Wolfe, Edgar Allen Poe, Abraham Lincoln, Johann Wolfgang von Goethe, Napoleon Bonaparte, Charles Dickens, Winston Churchill, Robert Schumann, Ludwig van Beethoven, Jack London, Charles Dickens, William Faulkner, Ernest Hemingway, Mark Twain, Rosemary Clooney, Florence Nightingale, Lord Byron, Alfred Lord Tennyson, Hermann Hesse, John Keats, Sylvia Plath, Hans Christian Andersen, Vivian Leigh,

Stephen Fry and Kurt Cobain. Of this very limited list alone three persons had committed suicide: Hemmingway, Plath and Cobain.

The symptoms of the manic episode of the disorder are as follows:

In mania, the patients exhibit a long period of feeling "high"— an overly happy or outgoing mood, but they are also irritable, feeling agitated, "jumpy" or "wired-up." During this episode, the patients talk at a very fast rate, jump from one idea to another, their thoughts are constantly racing, they are easily distracted and start new projects without much thought. In addition, they need only little sleep and exhibit an unrealistic belief in their abilities. As a result, they take part in a lot of pleasurable high-risk behaviors such as spending sprees, impulsive sex and risky business investments.

Patients with bipolar disorder also experience episodes of hypomania. During hypomanic episodes, the patient may have increased energy and creativity levels but these are not as severe as in typical mania and do not require emergency care. Patient in a hypomanic episode feels very well, are highly productive and functions well. They may not even feel that anything is wrong with them and only their family and friends can recognize their hypomanic symptoms. The hypomanic state does not last long and eventually converts into a manic or a depressive state.

Sometimes, a person with severe episodes of mania or depression may also experience psychotic symptoms such as hallucinations or delusions. As a result, such patients are sometimes wrongly diagnosed as having schizophrenia.

The symptoms of a depressive episode include the following: a long period of feeling worried or empty, a loss of all interest in activities once enjoyed (including sex), feeling tired or "slowed down", having problems concentrating, remembering and making decisions, being restless, sad or irritable, changing eating—sleeping—or other habits, thinking of death or suicide, or actually even attempting it.

Bipolar disorder is commonly treated with mood stabilizers such as Lithium and Valproic acid. Sometimes, antipsychotic—and antidepressant drugs are also used, along with the mood stabilizer. In general, patients continue treatment with mood stabilizers for years. But, as is the case with schizophrenia, many patients stop taking their drugs because of their very serious side-effects:

1. Lithium's side-effects include loss of coordination, excessive thirst, frequent urination, blackouts, seizures, slurred speech, fast or slow or irregular or pounding heartbeat, hallucinations, changes in vision, itching, rash, swelling of the eyes, face, lips, tongue, throat, hands, feet, ankles, or lower part of the legs.

2. Valproic acid's side-effects are changes in weight, nausea, stomach pain, vomiting, anorexia and loss of appetite. This drug can also cause damage to the liver or the pancreas.

Some of the patients stop taking their drugs for fear that they stem the pleasure and flow of the creativity that they experience during the hypomanic stage. Therefore, dear saviors," concluded Enid in a way that made us blush, "let us try to help these really miserable people."

Enid enrolled 78 outpatients that were in an active state of mania or depression at the time of the trial. As in the previous trials, one half of the patients, chosen at random, received soma inhalers and placebo pills that looked and tasted like their regular drugs and the other half received their regular true drug plus placebo inhalers.

The scientists entered the trial with some trepidation for 2 reasons:

A. Aside from the knowledge that bipolar disorder also has a genetic back-ground, the mechanism of its induction was still obscure.

B. The scientists were sure that the soma, because of its already proven efficiency, will help patients in the depression pole, but they were afraid that the soma might quickly cause them to switch from depression into a manic stage.

In spite of the group's misgivings, the soma worked beautifully! Even before opening the blind code, it became obvious that one half of the patients exhibited a complete cure! Enid and her staff were sure that they must belong to the soma group since they had never witnessed such miraculous cures before: patients in a manic episode moved from a manic to a hypomanic state in one day and within two additional days started to express the same serenity and bliss expected from an soma treatment. The depressive patients in this same half also became happy and serene after one or two days. At Enid's urgent behest and because of John's own impatience, the scientists hastily broke the double-blind code and were relieved and overjoyed to find that all the miraculous cures indeed happened in the soma group!

All the trial's patients, whether they were from the soma or Placebo groups, received 'take home' soma inhalers for 12 months. They were instructed to report back to the clinic during this period in case of unexplained reversals or unusual bad side-effects. No patient reported back early. As usual, all of the patients were told to prevent their relatives or friends from trying the soma, since it is extremely dangerous to "normal" people . . .

In one of the meetings that John and his group held with Enid, Debbie said: "Professor LeBlanc, I have heard a lot about patients who suffer from "split personalities" or DID (dissociative identity disorder) and during our Schizophrenia trial I learned from the Internet that this disorder should not be confused with schizophrenia. What, is it then?"

Enid said: "Dear Debbie, you have raised a very interesting and somewhat controversial issue; dissociative identity disorder (DID), which is also termed Multiple Personality Disorder (MPD), describes a condition in which a person displays multiple distinct identities or personalities known as" alter egos "or as "alters." Each "alter" has its own pattern of perceiving and interacting with the environment. Some psychiatrists maintain that DID does not actually exist as a valid medical diagnosis, whereas others think that it does exist. A third group maintains that DID exists, but is induced as a side-effect of psychological treatment. I have, at present, three DID women patients that I treat without worrying about the controversy that I just described.

The diagnosis of DID requires that at least two "alters" routinely take control of the individual's behavior and that each "alter" should not have any memory of the other "alters." These changes in identity, loss of memory and the awaking in unexplained locations and situations, cause a chaotic life. The incidence of DID is extremely low, but had gained exposure in episodes of crime-investigating television series where the culprit faked DID in order to escape punishment. DID patients demonstrate a variety of symptoms with wide fluctuations; their functioning can vary from severe impairment to normal or high abilities. Symptoms can include: attitudes and beliefs that differ across "alters", severe memory loss, depression, flashbacks of abuse/trauma, sudden anger without a justified cause, lack of intimacy and personal connections, frequent panic and anxiety attacks and auditory hallucinations of the "alters" inside their minds.

Different "alter" states may show distinct physiological changes and Electroencephalography (EEG) studies have shown distinct differences between alters in some subjects, while in other patients, the EEG patterns did not show such changes. Brain MRI studies have corroborated the transitions of identity in some DID sufferers. They have shown differing cerebral blood flows in the brain in different "alters" and distinct differences overall between DID patients and a healthy control group. One study in twins suggested that DID might have a genetic background since it was present in both twins.

A high percentage of patients reported child abuse. DID patients often report that they had experienced severe physical and sexual abuse during their childhood. Therefore, it was suggested that DID is strongly related to childhood trauma, rather than to an underlying electrophysiological dysfunction. Those psychologists who treat DID as a legitimate disorder, suggest the following mechanisms for its development: the child is harmed by a trusted caregiver (often a parent or guardian) and "splits off" the awareness and memory of the traumatic event in order to be able to survive in the damaging relationship. These "split off" memories and feelings go into the subconscious and are experienced later in the form of a separate personality. If the abuse happened repeatedly at different times, it causes the development of several "alters", each containing different memories and performing different functions. Thus, the DID becomes a coping mechanism for the individual when faced with further stressful situations.

However, as I have already mentioned, some investigators believe that the symptoms of DID are inadvertently created by therapists in suggestible patients upon using certain treatment techniques. The skeptics have observed that a small number of therapists are responsible for diagnosing the majority of persons with DID and that these patients did not report sexual abuse or manifested "alters" before treatment had begun, although this fact does really not prove much.

DID does not resolve spontaneously and the severity of the symptoms vary over time. With psychological treatment, patients with DID eventually recover.

As I have already told you, I have at present three women under treatment whose advance under psychotherapy is slow. What do you think John, shall we give them soma? The disorder has a very low occurrence rate, but all my patients are dear to me. John answered: "By all means, Enid. Even if the soma not cure their dissociative state, it may, at the very least, cure their depression."

Enid gave her patients soma inhalers for one month and stopped their psychological therapy during this month. A month later, the three women reported back and said that they feel great euphoria and calm and that their relatives have told them that during the last month they have exhibited only one "alter" that conformed to their own "true" original selves. Enid and the women's' therapist tested the women by trying to invoke their other "alters" under hypnosis, but none came to fore.

This success gave Enid another reason to regard John and his group as true "miracle workers" whose remedy is not the "snake oil" of con-men in the nineteenth century, but a real cure-all elixir! She said: "Dear friends, I know that several times I have embarrassed you with my 'hero worshiping' attitude...But you ought to realize that although I have reached the top of my profession, being a professor heading an important department, there had never been a single day in the past 30 years of my career that I did not rue my decision to specialize in Psychiatry. Surgeons and physicians in other branches of "physical" Medicine often achieve complete cures that I envy. In my line of work, complete successes and cures are too few. I see much anguish both in the patients and in their relatives, and I feel completely helpless. It is true that there are some useful drugs that treat various mental disorders, but as you know, many patients refuse to take them because of their side-effects. Now I am living through a wonderful period!

God bless you—you have made a not so young lady happy!

After completing the Bi-polar disorder trial, John and his group turned to tackle a very serious affliction – that of the Post Traumatic Stress Disorder (PTSD). John told his colleagues: "I am especially keen to try to cure PTSD patients, because of a personal reason. I think that I have already told you some time ago that my father suffers from PTSD. He participated in the Vietnam War as a USMC first lieutenant commanding a platoon. For his actions during the war, he was highly decorated, receiving a silver star, a bronze star and two purple Heart medals aside from several citations and various South Vietnamese medals. On release from the army, he was treated for PTSD in Boston with only little success. He once told me that he still experiences recurring terrible visions of some of his men being wounded or dying on the battlefield. He also said that he constantly suffers from a "survivor's guilt feeling" of being alive when many of his men died, possibly as a result of faulty combat decisions that he might have made. In addition, he could not understand the disdain that people in the US felt for the Vietnam War combatants who were told upon enlistment that they are going to fight for their country and for democracy. I think that it is shameful that veterans of unpopular conflicts such as the Vietnam War, have been often blamelessly criticized. When we started with the soma trials, it had long been my intention to enroll my father as a subject in a PTSD trial."

To perform the trial, John called Enid and found that she and her staff do not treat PTSD patients in their ward or outpatient clinic. She told John to contact PTSD experts in the veterans' Affairs (VA) Healthcare System in Boston. She said that this system consists of a set of hospitals run by the United States Department of Veterans Affairs and offers both physical and mental health treatments in several locations. Of these Bostonian campuses, Enid recommended that they will contact the Winchester campus which has a nationally known PTSD—and drug-abuse program that is managed by a colleague of hers, Dr. William Trent. She said that Dr. Trent's program tries to help men and women veterans develop skills, to maintain drug abstinence, and to manage PTSD symptoms. Enid was sure that Dr. Trent will be very happy to carry out a soma trial with them and promised to help with Dr. Trent if need should arise.

As was their habit before starting a trial, Ben, Debbie and Lucia consulted the Internet site of the National Institutes of Mental Health, in order to learn more about the disorder (John was already quite knowledgeable about it). This is what they read:

"PTSD is an anxiety disorder that can develop after exposure to a terrifying event or ordeal in which grave physical harm occurred, or was threatened. Traumatic events that may trigger PTSD include violent physical or sexual assaults, domestic violence, natural or human-caused disasters, abuse, accidents, or military combat. PTSD caused by military combat had been termed "shell shock" in past wars.

When in danger, it's natural to feel afraid. This fear triggers many split-second changes in the body that are needed to defend it against the danger or to avoid it – the so called "fight-or-flight" response. In PTSD, this reaction acquires an additional aspect: people who have PTSD may feel stressed or frightened even when they're no longer in danger. Anyone can get PTSD at any age. Moreover, not everyone with PTSD has been through a dangerous event. Some people get PTSD after a friend or family member experienced danger or was harmed. The sudden, unexpected death of a loved one can also cause PTSD.

According to information supplied by the National Institute of Mental Health, about 15% of men and 10% of women among Vietnam veterans were found to suffer from PTSD. Many of them still suffer from terrible nightmares causing them to wake up in shrieks, drenched with cold sweat. In addition, it is estimated that several millions of American adults of the age of 18 and older have or had PTSD after violent personal assaults. PTSD can cause many symptoms. These symptoms can be grouped into three categories:

1. Re-experiencing symptoms and flashbacks — re-living the trauma over and over again, including having physical symptoms like a racing heart or sweating and frightening

thoughts. Re-experiencing symptoms may cause problems in a person's everyday routine: just words, objects, or situations that are reminders of the traumatic event, can trigger re-experiencing.

2. Avoidance symptoms: staying away from places, events, or objects that are reminders of the experience. For example, after a bad car accident, a person who usually drives may avoid driving or riding in a car.

3. Hyper-arousal symptoms: being easily startled, feeling tense or "on edge", having difficulty sleeping and/or having angry outbursts. Hyper-arousal symptoms are usually continuous, instead of being triggered by things that remind one of the traumatic events. They can make the person feel stressed and angry. These symptoms may make it hard for the patient to perform daily tasks.

It's natural to have some of the symptoms after a dangerous event and people may have very serious symptoms that go away after a few weeks. This is called acute stress disorder, or ASD. But, when the symptoms last more than a few weeks and become an ongoing problem, the persons might have PTSD.

In addition to the symptoms described above, PTSD patients also suffer from bad depression and sadness, anxiety and Alcohol or drug addictions. The Alcohol and drugs are used to still the "demons" that continuously haunt them. Patients may also feel suicidal. The memorable portrayal of a crippled and Alcoholic Vietnam war veteran, "lieutenant Dan", portrayed by actor Gary Sinise in "Forrest Gump", is an excellent illustration of a PTSD stricken war veteran who at one time in the movie wanted to commit suicide."

After they read all they could, John told his group: "dear friends, as you know, many PTSD patients also have drug abuse problems. However, when we run our trial, we shall choose patients without drug problems. Thus, we shall be able to study the-soma effect on PTSD alone, dissociated from drug addiction. However, regardless of whether the -Soma will cure or not cure PTSD, our next trial tackle drug addiction."

John and his group contacted the Winchester center's director, Dr. Wiliam Trent and described to him their past successes with the mental disorders that they had already studied so far. Dr. Trent was very happy to start a trial with what seemed like to him like an excellent psychiatric drug. John asked Dr. Trent to enroll only patients who are free of drug addictions (verifiable by repeated urine tests) explaining that he eventually plans to run a separate clinical trial on Heroin addicts that do not suffer from PTSD.

When starting to plan the trial, Dr. Trent suggested that it will contain three arms: one group of patients will receive soma inhalers and undergo their regular psychiatric treatment sessions; another group will receive placebo inhalers and will also undergo the same psychiatric treatment, and the third group receive placebo inhalers and be treated with the psychiatric Prolonged Exposure (PE) method developed by Professor Edna Foa. He said that Professor Foam from the University of Pennsylvania's Center for the Treatment and Study of Anxiety and the Department of Psychiatry in the School of Medicine, developed a successful therapy for PTSD patients that involved identifying the thoughts and situations that had triggered fear in each patient, and then gently exposing the patients to those situations: the patients are asked to summon up the memories and the images associated with the trauma more and more vividly. Following that, the patients are gently exposed to films of combat or car accidents or any other frightening situation that triggered their PTSD. The facing of the frightening memories and images gradually stripped them of their debilitating power. The approach works fast— usually within a structured program of 12 sessions. The patients are also provided with education about PTSD and are taught a breathing control method for helping them to manage anxiety.

Dr. Trent told the group that the US Department of Veterans Affairs had put Professor Foa's treatment protocol into wide use and that it is now implementing programs to teach it to mental health therapists of the VA across the various services.

John said: "Dr. Trent, if Professor Foa's approach is so successful, why do you need the -?"

Dr Trent answered: "We need the -Cip hopefully, for two reasons: many PTSD patients are very reluctant to open old people that are a must in Foa's method and also, much more importantly, we need to treat many thousands of patients, but I have in my clinic at present only three qualified therapists who had attended Professor Foa's courses. No, a drug which will cure every one of the many thousands of PTSD veteran patients in the country without a need for hundreds of qualified therapists, and without much hassle, is extremely necessary!"

Dr Trent enrolled forty-eight non-addicted PTSD veterans that came regularly to the clinic for psychiatric treatments but, as yet, had not received any PE treatments. These veterans were randomly divided into three groups with an approximately similar division of ages and wars (Vietnam, Iraq and Afghanistan). The groups were assigned the letters "A", "B" or "C." John and his group coded 16 placebo inhalers with the letter "A" and revealed to Dr. Trent and his clinicians that these are placebo inhalers intended for the PE treatment group. Next, they coded sixteen -Cip inhalers with the letter "B" and sixteen additional placebo inhalers with the letter "C." The identities of the "B" and "C" inhalers were withheld from Dr. Trent and his staff. All the psychiatric treatments (PE for group A patients, or conventional – for groups "B" and "C" patients) were to be administered by Dr. Trent's three PE qualified clinicians at a rate of two sessions per week. This way, all 48 patients were to undergo a total of twelve sessions (for thirty-two of them—a regular psychiatric treatment, and for the other sixteen—the twelve sessions required by the PE method). Dr. Trent did not participate in the trial, since he had not taken the PE course and also because he had his usual managerial duties and the task of supervising the whole trial. John asked Dr. Trent to enroll his dad as one the 16 patients of "B" or "C" groups. He told his dad that he may not feel any improvement in the six weeks of the trial, since he has a 50% chance of being placed in the placebo group. But he told his dad that if the soma will work, he will be entitled, officially, to receive the soma after the end of the trial. John's father was already well aware of his son's previous successes with the soma and willingly joined the trial.

At the end of each week of the trial, John and his group, and Dr. Trent and his clinicians met for a follow-up session. Starting with the first week, the three clinicians, without knowing the identity of the "B" or "C" groups, described an amazing progress in group B patients – they were happier, serene and reported a general improvement in all mental aspects of their life. The patients of the PE Group "A" exhibited a certain regression in their mental condition at the start, but this was expected in the PE treatment due to the surfacing of all the experiences they had tried so hard to suppress (a real improvement in Professor Foa's method, is expected to appear only after 8 or 9 sessions). Group "C" placebo patients expected an improvement in their condition because of the trial, and therefore reported a slight placebo-like improvement. But this "improvement" had soon dissipated as the trial went on. As a result, Dr. Trent and his clinicians said that they believe that they already know the exact identity of groups "B" and "C" members, but did not press John to break the code.

The results of the clinical trial were tremendously successful. Most PE patients reported a strong improvement; the soma patients were cured and were both ecstatic and serene, while the placebo patients remained with their unresolved PTSD. At the end of the trial, all forty-eight patients, including those who recovered as a result of the PE treatment, received soma inhalers for one month and were told that they will routinely receive a new inhaler at the beginning of each month for one year (John left enough inhalers for a whole year's supply with Dr. Trent, hoping that the soma will be certified by the FDA after one year). The patients also received the usual Ben's concocted warning. Only one year later, when the -Cip was openly distributed to the whole world, they understood the reason for the warnings that they had received...

While the PTSD trial was still progressing, John assembled his group and said: "Dear colleagues, the time has come for us to try to abolish drug addiction. Our next trial will be carried out on Heroin abusers that are trying to undergo a "drying-out" process in one of the Drug Dependency Treatment Centers in Boston. Now, I will have you know that I have served for a while as a Pharmacology expert in a special committee for drug abuse and treatment which had been established by the governor of Massachusetts and therefore, I studied the Heroin addiction problem quite extensively. It is true that we have committees, programs and centers galore all over the country. However, Heroin addiction is most difficult to eradicate, even with replacement therapies with drugs such as Methadone and Buprenorphine. Both of these drugs alleviate Heroin's very torturous withdrawal symptoms. But the wish to reexperience Heroin "highs" is still present, and it takes a very strong-willed individual to resist the psychological urge to regress back to addiction. All addictive drugs, including Heroin and Alcohol (which we shall tackle later in another clinical trial), stimulate a reward circuit in the brain. The circuit provides incentives for abuse by registering the rewarding and pleasurable experiences through the release of the dopamine, telling the brain "To do it again." Therefore, what makes permanent recovery difficult are drug-induced changes that create lasting memories linking the drug to a pleasurable reward.

When I started my tenure as adviser to the governor's committee, I asked my dad what he knew about drug abuse in Vietnam, which was the harbinger of the Heroin abuse of to-day. He told me that Marijuana, Amphetamines, Opium and Heroin were almost openly used in Vietnam without any extensive legal persecution by the army. In a battalion-briefing on drug abuse among soldiers that he attended in 1968 with his fellow officers, they were told that 50 percent of American servicemen "do" drugs and the officers were given instructions to try to fight this problem. American intelligence sources received many reports that the Vietcong secretly exported drugs into the south in order to undermine American morale and their wish to fight. Notoriously similar technics were used by

England, and other western countries using opium smuggling into China, during their attempt to open trade with her, by force. By the year 1970, when my dad was released from the army, the percentage of drug users among servicemen had jumped to 65%. My Dad also said that drugs in Vietnam were both cheap and easily available and were a way for the soldiers to escape from the anxiety and stress of combat. He told me that in 1967 opium cost 1 dollar, while morphine was sold for 5 dollars per vial. Tablets of Binoctal, an addictive drug, were sold at 1—to 5—dollars for twenty tablets. Heroin was widely available to U.S troops and was smoked (not injected) in the following way: a regular cigarette was rolled between the finger and thumb to loosen its tobacco. After the cigarette was partially emptied, a vial containing 250 milligrams of 94 to 96 percent pure heroin liquid was poured into it. Often, the widespread heroin use among U.S. servicemen in Vietnam was caused by starting with marijuana and then "graduating" to heroin abuse.

Heroin is processed from morphine, a naturally occurring substance extracted from the seed pods of certain varieties of poppy plants. It is typically sold as a white or brownish powder, or as a black sticky substance known in the streets as "black tar heroin." Although purer heroin is becoming more common, most street heroin is "cut" with other drugs or with substances such as sugar, starch, powdered milk, or quinine. Heroin causes a very strong and rapid surge in the levels of the three neurotransmitters which affect the reward system in the brain, thereby causing addiction. The brain remembers this pleasure and wants it repeated.

The addicts' need to obtain Heroin becomes more important than any other need, including truly vital necessities like eating. The drive to seek and use the drug is all that matters, despite devastating consequences. Finally, self-control, freedom of choice and everything that once held value in a person's life—family, job and community—are lost to addiction. As addiction sets in, several changes occur in the brain. The most significant among them is a reduction in the production of the pleasure receptors in the brain. As a result, the addict is incapable of feeling any pleasure, even when he greatly increases his Heroin intake. If Heroin's use is reduced or stopped abruptly, grave withdrawal symptoms occur. These withdrawal symptoms occur within a few hours after the drug was stopped and include restlessness, muscle and bone pain, insomnia, diarrhea, vomiting, cold flashes with goose bumps and involuntary leg movements. The withdrawal symptoms peak between 24 and 48 hours after the last dose and subside after about a week. Heroin withdrawal is never fatal to otherwise healthy adults, but it causes a great deal of suffering.

One of the greatest risks of being a Heroin addict is death from heroin overdose. As a result of the fact that with time, "normal" doses of Heroin fail to induce pleasure, addicts continuously increase their uptake. Consequently, about one percent of all heroin addicts in the United States die each year from an overdose of Heroin, despite their development of fantastic tolerance to high concentrations of the drug.

Because many heroin addicts, including whores, often share needles and injection equipment, they are at a special risk of contracting HIV, Hepatitis and other infectious diseases and passing them on. Drug abuse is the fastest growing vector for the spread of HIV and Hepatitis in the Nation.

How can an addict achieve drug abstinence and overcome the hump of withdrawal symptoms? It is possible to stop "cold turkey" – that is without the help of withdrawal drugs – but, it creates very painful withdrawal symptoms. Another mode of relieving the withdrawal symptoms of Heroin addicts at the start of abstinence is to sedate them heavily for 2-4 days.

At present, the best mode of treatment of Heroin addiction and dependence consists of creating a sort of "narcotic blockade" that stops the craving for the drug. This so called "maintenance agonist treatment" uses one or the other of two medications (agonists) called Methadone and Buprenorphine. These two medications have cross tolerance with Heroin and Morphine and a long duration effect. Both Methadone and Buprenorphine work equally well.

Let us start with the description of Methadone treatment: high doses of methadone can block the euphoric effects of heroin, morphine and similar drugs and can also prevent withdrawal symptoms. As a result, properly—dosed methadone patients who persist in the maintenance of the agonist treatment can overcome the painful withdrawal symptoms and later can also resist their craving.

Methadone maintenance therapy has many years of proven efficacy. It increases overall survival, treatment retention and employment. It decreases Heroin use, criminal activity, prostitution and hepatitis/HIV infections. The treatment is given in clinics and involves daily dosing and nursing assessments, weekly individual and/or group counseling, random urine screenings and psychiatric services. These daily visits to the clinic can be very tiresome to treated addicts. However, individuals can eventually earn 'take-home' doses for a whole week if they have met the goals of the program long enough.

Buprenorphine is the second maintenance therapy drug: it

has been shown to be just as effective as methadone in terms of abstinence, continuation of treatment and decreased craving.

The choice between Methadone and Buprenorphine depends on the addict's situation. If he needs a constantly supportive structure, methadone is the better choice. As I have already told you, the goal of both drugs is to alleviate acute craving, but the patients will still continue to crave Heroin, since they remember the acute pleasure, they felt at the start of their addiction.

I am fairly certain that the prevent addicts from sliding back into abuse, since they can now actually gain pleasure in a safe and easy administration route. They will be able to obtain the soma free of charge from the DEA once it is certified. The soma will also have an additional advantage, since its pleasure-inducing ability will not diminish over time and will not cause any adverse side-effects."

John finished his long tirade, picked up the phone and asked Dr. Trent to recommend a Drug Dependency Treatment Center in the Boston area. Dr. Trent suggested that they should try the VA Substance Abuse outpatient Treatment Service in Channel Street which specializes in Methadone treatment. Dr. Trent also said that he will call the center's manager, Dr. Perez, who is a friend of his and will prepare the ground for them. As soon as John put down the phone, which was in a speaker mode, Ben remarked that "It looks like all the psychiatrists and psychologists in Boston seem to be entwined in a "Mafia-style" network where a friend brings a friend." John laughed and reminded Ben that he, John, also belongs to the same Mafia and warned him to behave, or else he will find a decapitated horse head in his bedroom as a result of his insult to the "psychologists' Mafia"...

John and his group met Dr. Perez in the latter's office, described their successful results with the soma and offered to carry out a trial with him. Dr. Perez, already briefed by Dr. Trent, immediately agreed and they started to discuss the way to perform the trial.

A few days later, Dr. Perez assembled 42 Methadone-treated veterans in the clinic's conference room and said: "men and women veterans; The course you are taking now with Methadone is not easy and I know that you constantly have to fight the urge to slide back to Heroin abuse to regain at least a temporary pleasure. But now your agonies may be over. I have met a group of brilliant scientists from Harvard University who have developed a new, marvelous, addiction-free and pleasure-inducing drug that will replace both Heroin and Methadone. I have invited you to-day to participate in a trial with this new drug. Those who would consider taking part please stay and I shall describe the new drug and will answer any questions you may want to ask. You also need to know that, as is the custom in clinical trials, half of you will receive the new drug and the other half will receive a placebo. However, if the soma will work, as I am sure that it will, all of you, including the placebo group people, will receive the drug free of charge for a whole year." All present, without any exception, agreed to enroll in the trial and signed informed consent forms. Dr. Perez patiently answered all their questions and then said: "The drug or the placebo will be administered with an inhaler of the same type used by asthma patients. You will take one whiff per day from your inhaler which delivers only a single, but accurate, dose per day when you press the piston. Later I shall demonstrate to you the correct method of inhalation using a placebo inhaler. Both the true drug and the placebo will suffice exactly for one month. In addition, those of the placebo group will receive enough Methadone doses for one month to take together with the inhalers, whereas the real new drug takers will receive placebo doses that look and taste exactly like Methadone. You will report back to the clinic after one month and will be interviewed about your experience with the drug. You may tell your families about the trial, but you will need to swear them to secrecy.

It is very important that you should not tell any of your friends about the trial and don't let them try the inhaler which contains an exact number of whiffs for one month. If you let anybody else use the inhaler, you will miss doses at the end of the month and will suffer very painful withdrawal symptoms from the lack of the drug.

Dr. Perez demonstrated the correct use of the inhaler and put the list of the coded soma or placebo users in his safe.

The trial was extremely successful. The scientists and Dr. Perez knew that they have gained, at last, an extremely important victory in the war against drug addiction. Although John and his group had only tested Heroin addiction, they were quite sure that the soma will also work on all abuse drugs in general, since almost all illegal street drugs work with the same type of receptor as that of soma and Heroin. Thus, John and his group added a very important "scalp" to the collection that they have accumulated so far on their belts...

CHAPTER 14

The performance of an anti-violence trial under the auspices of the U.N.

RAVI MEENAKSHI CONVENED THE UN General Assembly to a special emergency session. Prior to the session which, according to the secretary, was going to astound the whole world, the press Secretary of the United Nations asked for and received coverage from most of the major TV stations in the world. The secretary allowed two days for preparation, advertising and public relations. During these two days, newspaper and TV correspondents all over the world speculated about the possible reason for the special emergency session: "aliens from outer space contacted the UN, considering it to be the governing authority of all earth ("take me to your leader!"), or that scientists have discovered an ultimate drug for all types of cancer, or god forbid, a very lethal virus was discovered in some remote corner in the world and is extremely contagious and incurable" and so on... Bookies all over the world started bets on the soma, which is going to revolutionize the whole world! The SOMA is a non-addictive happiness—and serenity-inducing drug that can also cure all human mental disorders and all forms of depression! This drug is going to bring real "peace in our time" to the whole world—not like the "peace" achieved in 1938 by Neville Chamberlain, Great Britain's prime minister, by allowing

Hitler to conquer Poland... We are sponsoring this wonderful drug will distribute it throughout the whole world.

Very recently, many people the world have been utterly amazed by a very happy political event in Sudan: after long and terrible civil wars, all the fighting parties in Darfur and the Sudanese government have finally signed a comprehensive peace treaty. This tremendous achievement was secretly instigated by us! We gave the fighters by subterfuge to all the fighting parties in Darfur and it transformed all combatants into euphoric, serene and peace-loving people! Based on this tremendous success, we are going to distribute the soma to the whole world, thus achieving the great aim of the UN to bring peace. Billions of doses of this drug have already been secretly manufactured by the non-profit "climate" consortium of Bill Kelly and Warren Brooks that ostensibly pretended to try to reduce all greenhouse gases in the atmosphere!" The secretary stopped his address for a few seconds to let his words sink in, but could not continue: all the ambassadors to the UN and the heads of all governments that attended the plenary session rose up as one man and applauded. The secretary then called me, my group and Bill and Warren to the podium to share the accolades. The secretary continued: "Dear citizens of the world, the soma will be distributed, free of charge, to everybody through our World Food Program (WFP). Many additional centers will be established soon, in order to distribute the soma all over the world."

At the start, not all citizens of the world agreed to try the soma. The more cautious and paranoid ones among them waited to see what will happen. But soon all flocked to the many WFP distribution centers in each country to receive it. With time, the

WFP was re-directed to distributing food and the UN established "UNSA" – the United Nations Agency—to distribute the soma.

As the sole distributor, The UN now wielded enormous power over the whole world and boycotted several countries: those that supported terrorist activities, produced weapons of mass destruction and that were ruled by corrupt dictators who exploited and abused their people. The ban on these black-list countries yielded immediate and impressive results: their citizens rebelled and ousted their belligerent corrupt governments and dictators in order to join the happy and peaceful family of all the world's nations. At long last, all the countries that had possessed nuclear weapons, dangerous warfare germs and toxic gases quickly destroyed them! In 2013 there were about 250 disputes and war sites in the world, and in 2014 the number dwindled to zero. This happy outcome led to a motion by all governments and countries in the world to create an UN-administered world government and thus, out of many nations, came one world government whose moto was "E pluribus unum – out of many (nations) one (world government)!"

CHAPTER 15

Chapter x: The broadcasting of the Nobel prize awarding

IN SPITE OF THE DIFFERENT time zones in the Globe, billions of TV sets were turned-on in countless apartments and houses, Kazakh Yurts, Mongolian Gers, African thatch-covered clay huts, Eskimo Igloos, astrodomes on the moon and in various other types of human habitats. The sets were tuned to the news channels which were going to broadcast live, courtesy of WBR-TV Boston, a special address by Professor John Novick, the world's savior. To watch this broadcast in real time, men, women and children gathered in front of their sets even though it was late at night or very early in the morning in some time zones. Within every Tri-D Holovision "cube", the WBR-TRI-D newscaster was seen speaking and his words were simultaneously translated into the various languages and dialects of all countries in the world.

The newscaster said: "WBR-TV is thankful for the privilege of bringing to you a historical broadcast of great importance – an address by Professor John Novick, the famous co-inventor of the soma drug. During his address you will also see his three colleagues who accompanied him during the process of development of the soma and will continue to work with him at Harvard – his partner to the two Nobel prizes Professor Benjamin Fond, Dr. Debra Cohen and his pharmacist technician Mrs. Lucia Fernandez. As you know,

Professor Novick and his colleagues refused until now, to make public appearances other than the one they made at the Nobel Prize Ceremony. They did not want to be recognized on every outing and approached by grateful citizens. However, in the wake of countless entreaties from around the world, including from UN's General Secretary, Ravi Meenakshi, Professor Novick agreed to address the world, choosing WBR-Tri-D in Boston as his venue.

Until professor Novick starts, we will show you slides containing the announcements of both the Swedish Nobel Prize committee for Medicine or Physiology and the Norwegian Nobel Peace Prize committee on the winners for year 2014. We will allow enough time for the various stations around the world to translate them."

The Royal Swedish Academy of Sciences

6 October 2014, Stockholm,

Press Release

The Royal Swedish Academy of Sciences has decided to award the Nobel Prize in Medicine or Physiology for 2014, jointly, to John Novick and to Benjamin Fond from the Department of Neurochemistry, Harvard University School of Medicine for their invention of the happiness-inducing soma drug. This drug cured mental disorders that affected many people in the past – and, most importantly, brought great happiness and serenity to all humanity.

For the first time in the history of prizes, all the members of the Academy, unanimously and enthusiastically, voted for the two winning candidates of this year. All members believed that there had never been a single invention in modern times that had such an impact on the welfare and health of humanity like the soma. Moreover, our committee had to argue with the Nobel Peace Prize committee on the sole right for awarding the Prize. Finally, a compromise has been reached whereby both committees will award the prizes. This illustrates how important is Professors Novick's and Fond's contribution to the world.

Den Norske Nobelcomite
Oslo, October 9, 2014

The Norwegian Nobel Peace Prize Committee has decided that the Prize for 2014 is to be awarded to: Professors John Novick and Benjamin Fond from the Department of Neurochemistry, Harvard University School of Medicine for their success in bringing Peace to the world with the happiness-inducing drug that they have invented. This drug has brought peace, freedom from depression and oppression and great happiness to all people in the world. It successfully eliminated all wars, terrorist activities and conflicts in the globe. The peace that we are now enjoying what may be justly called "Paxtica". By awarding the prize to these scientists, the committee wishes to express the world's gratitude for their great contribution to the future and the welfare of Mankind.

The newscaster continued: "It is worth mentioning that never before had two Nobel Prizes been awarded to the same person in the same year. Since the establishment of the Prizes, four persons had been awarded two Nobel Prizes: Mary Curie won the prize for Physics for discovering radioactivity in 1903 and the Prize in Chemistry for the discovery of Radium in 1913; Linus Pauling won the Prize for Chemistry in 1954 for elucidating the nature of Chemical bonds and the peace Prize in 1962 for his action against above-ground Nuclear Bomb testing; John Bardeen won two prizes in Physics: for the discovery of the Transistor in 1956 and for the development of the theory of Super-conductivity in 1972; Frederick Sanger received 2 Prizes in Chemistry: for elucidating the complete amino acid sequence of Insulin in 1958 and for developing techniques for nucleic acid sequencing in 1980.

Then the newscaster said: "our channel controller signals that Professor Novick's address is about to start, so here it is":

The image of the newscaster faded and that of Professor Novick appeared: "Dear Viewers, we are lucky to live in a blissful world that the children in the audience probably believe had always been happy. But, until the invention of the soma, our world was immersed in a mire of depression, sadness and wars. Whole populations in many countries were poor and in grave danger to their lives. Even in the more affluent and strong countries there were men, women and children who suffered from depression and mental disorders and almost never experienced happiness.

Before the invention of the soma, well-wishing and wise people from various fields tried to alleviate depression: Men of religion tried to console and to instill hope in the depressed. Shamans and Faith-Healers tried to drive away depression by rituals, incantations and various medicinal herbs. Spiritual and mystic organizations advocated that depressed people must redeem their sins from past incarnations and after suffering in their present one, will gain everlasting peace and Nirvana after their death.

Psychologists tried to elucidate the cause of unhappiness and depression and to find the means to overcome it. Sigmund Freud, for example, maintained that Man's prime drive is to strive for pleasure and that those who failed in this striving, react by developing depression. Another noted Psychologist, Alfred Adler, believed that humans crave power and control and that their depression is the result of their failure to achieve it. Another opinion was expressed by Viktor Frankl, a survivor of a German concentration camp. In his 1946 book "Man's search for meaning" he stated that Man's prime motivation is to find meaning and significance in his life. He claimed that many people are trapped in an existential vacuum – a lack of a sense of purpose and direction. Frankl suggested that every man should overcome this existential vacuum by finding meaning in his life and targets to achieve. As a result of the findings of these and other sages, psychological treatments were devised that can, partly, alleviate depression. However, these psychological treatments may take years to succeed and are expensive. In my opinion, psychotherapy mostly succeeds in cases where the patients underwent painful traumas during their birth, infancy, childhood or adulthood. For others, the benefit of "shrinking" may be only marginal.

In Genesis 6:5 of the King James Version, we find the following verse:

"And God saw that the wickedness of man was great in the earth and that every imagination of the thoughts of his heart was only evil continually."

This verse was echoed in age-old philosophical discussions on the root of all evil and the sad situation of the Human Condition. Scientists now claim that "evil" derives from our primitive reptilian brain. In some extremely evil people such as dictators and sociopathic criminals, the strong and continuous output of this primitive brain is not prevented or sublimated by the control of their higher brain, the Neocortex (which is responsible for higher-order thinking skills, reason, speech, judgment, abstract thinking, imagination and intelligence). Following the administration of our soma to all people in the world, we proved that the age-old claim that "the wickedness of man was great in the earth and that the thoughts of his heart was only evil continually" is not true at all:

euphoric and serene people are not evil – they are generous and considerate unto others ..

With regards to depression, its causes and the ways to alleviate it, I believed that only a pharmacological-biochemical approach can cure depression! I maintained that the Great Creator, or Nature and Evolution if you will made us biologically and psychologically vulnerable. We are not armored like turtles or partly immune to cancer or diseases like sharks, or long-lived like the Galapagos tortoises. We have a developed brain, an opposing thumb which helps us to hold objects and the subtlest and most adept vocal organs of all species that allowed us to develop speech. But our minds are sensitive and vulnerable. Our brain resembles a complex computer that may contain bugs due to problems encountered during pregnancy and birth, or it can be affected by neurological, genetic and developmental defects that may cause mental disorders and depression. Neurochemists in recent years have proved that depression is caused by an imbalance (excess, or scarcity) of important biochemical compounds in the brain. They believed, as I did, that almost every person can be cured of his/her depression or mental disorder if we shall re-adjust his brain's biochemical equilibrium. We ought to remember that men (aside from their "souls" and emotions) are no more than complex biochemical structures made from the atoms of Mendeleyev's periodic table of elements.... Therefore, my colleagues and I were quite sure that the recent breakthroughs in brain research, genetic engineering, neurochemistry and pharmacology ought to lead to the development better anti-depressant drugs than those that existed at the start of our research.

Luckily for Humanity, my colleagues and I succeeded in our

quest. As you know, we developed an anti-depressant drug which was extremely efficient, much beyond our wildest dreams and expectations!

Professor Fond and I won two Nobel Prizes for the year 2014. In my Nobel Prize address in Stockholm, I said that I consider myself to be no more than a competent scientist who got lucky ..... and since I am a science-fiction fan, I also said that perhaps some higher entities planted the idea of the soma research in my sub-consciousness. I carried this "idea" even further and said that perhaps these entities wanted to save Humanity at the twelfth hour before we shall annihilate each other in an atomic war or by chemical and microbiological warfare... Indeed, after watching documentary films from the past, I am amazed to see how depressing and frightening were world news before the soma. Now, in contrast, people are so considerate, peaceful and compassionate, helping those in need, and abandoning all their earlier paths of greed, corruption, oppression and wars.

Therefore, every day and night I give praise in humble gratitude to all possible addresses – God, sublime entities, angels, aliens, collective—or my own subconscious mind that, perhaps, helped me to conceive the idea of the soma.

Those who would like to know more about the course of development of our soma are invited to read the book that Professor Ben Fond, Dr. Debra Cohen and I wrote: 'The road to happiness – the invention of the soma'. It can also be found in the Internet at "www.com." This site contains translations of the book to almost all the major languages."

Dear viewers I received Nobel prizes in 2014. I received the Prize for Medicine or Physiology in the concert hall of Stockholm, Sweden, from King Karl Gustav the 16th also for Professor Fond; while Dr. Fond received the Nobel peace prize, also on my behalf, from king Harald the 5th at the municipality house in Oslo, Norway. Let me describe to you "my" Nobel prize awarding ceremony in Stockholm: on each day during the Nobel week, one of the prize winners of that year gave a public address – the "Nobel lecture"—describing the work which earned him, or her, the prize. Finally, the day of the presentation of the prizes came. The presentation ceremony was conducted in the presence of the king, his family, honored guests, the members of the various Nobel Prize committees and relatives of the winners (including my wife Dr. Debra Cohen, my parents and my sister. Ben's family accompanied him to Oslo. Many Nobel laureates from past years also attended. Presentation speeches were given by various Swedish scientists – experts in field of each prize—praising the laureates and their discovery. Following that, His Majesty the King of Sweden handed each winner a diploma and a medal. The Ceremony was followed by a banquet at the Stockholm City Hall for about 1,300 people where the winners, one representative from each category, delivered their acceptance speech (also termed "banquet speech"). The reason that I am describing this ceremony to you is not to brag about it, but to present my somewhat perplexing acceptance speech and give you some food for thought …John spoke first, and this is what he said:

"Your Majesty, Your Royal Highness, Mr. President of the royal Swedish academy, Excellencies, Ladies and Gentlemen: Many Nobel laureates made inspiring and exciting speeches in this magnificent hall and, therefore, I will have to try my utmost to measure up to their high standards. I am a Science Fiction and Fantasy fan, and therefore I want to tell you a story that could, perhaps, shed light on how the idea of the development of the soma may have evolved in my mind. Is my story real, or is it just a dream that I had? I myself, do not know... Since we constantly enjoy the benefits of the soma, why should we really care how it came into being? Still, here it is:

About 79 earth-time years ago, a committee convened in one of the planets of our galaxy. This committee, whose formal name was "The galactic committee for the preservation of young sentient races", was made of several members of highly developed races that we call "extraterrestrial aliens" in Science-Fiction novels. The job of this committee was to locate sentient races in the galaxy that reached the ability to perform nuclear fission but as yet had not reached enlightenment and world peace, and to prevent them from blowing up their planets. The committee was convened in the wake of detection of nuclear explosions in New-Mexico and Japan. This committee, whose experience was immense in this kind of task, exercised various covert means to achieve their objective— they snatched humans into their spaceship, studied their anatomy, physiology and brain. These human guinea pigs were eventually returned befuddled to earth after a day or two with vague memories of aliens studying them. No wonder that there have been increasing reports in the last decades of alien UFOs in our atmosphere and of people claiming that they have been snatched by aliens... The committee studied the various neurotransmitters in the human brain and came to the conclusion that the administration of soma to humans will turn them into moral and serene beings and will eliminate all feelings of greed, belligerency and depression. They have already used similar techniques successfully on other young sentient races in the galaxy that had different chemistries, but had responded favorably to the administration of our Anti-Depressant drug.

Consequently, the members of the committee searched around for a neurochemist that was living alone, as I was at that time, and that could advance the development of a peace-inducing drug. As a result, the aliens drugged me, snatched me up to their spaceship and instilled the idea of the in my brain. This may be why before the actual start of our soma research I had from time to time, recurring strange dreams of aliens speaking to telepathically. Then one morning I woke up with the whole soma project mapped out in my brain. On coming to my office in the morning, I immediately started to draft a grant proposal to the National institute of mental health for the development of an anti-depressant free of side-effects. I ought to mention that, luckily for the world, I was the best suitable candidate for such research since even before the aliens' intervention I had studied and its effects quite extensively in my lab.

"Your Majesty, Your Royal Highness, Mr. President, Excellencies, Ladies and Gentlemen. This is my story. Accept or reject it if you wish. In fact, I am not even sure, myself, if it is real or just a hallucination or a dream that I have experienced." The audience sat fascinated and did not know whether to accept my story at face value, or just as a beautiful fairy tale or jest.

Then I added: "whether or not my story is true, I want to sing hosannas to the soma:

It made us serene, euphoric, loving and happy;

It cured all Humanity's mental diseases;

It strengthened our immune system and improved our general health;

125

It eradicated all crime from the world;

It stopped all wars, terrorist activities and conflicts between nations;

It eradicated all greed, racism and hunger and made us all charitable to one another;

It united us under a single world government and eliminated all chauvinism and narrow nationalism.

Finally, I would like to address the Nobel peace prize committee in Oslo: I have read the regulations of the nominating Nobel Prize committees and learned that each Nobel Prize laureate has the privilege of nominating candidates for next year's Nobel prizes. Although Bill Kelly and Warren Brooks had already won many acclaims, medals and accolades all over the world, in my opinion it is still not enough Therefore, I would like to nominate them as candidates for next year's Nobel peace prize. Without them the soma might not have come into being."

John completed his television address and said: "Dear viewers, this is the end of my address. I would like to bid all of you a happy soma day or night, as the case may be in your time zones. Have a happy life and prosper and may God bless you all!"

Thus, the epic broadcast came to its end. The newscaster thanked all the translators and the WBR-TV personnel, and his face faded out from the television screen."

Dear readers,

You probably wonder whether the research outline that I drew in the book is only fictional or is scientifically sound. The answer is that this research plan is, indeed, feasible. A neurotransmitter that alleviates pain and induces euphoria and the methods that I "invented" for its production and administration are scientifically possible. However, even if the SOMA would actually work in humans, its action can be only short-lived. SOMA's receptors (which are also common to other Opioid drugs) are bound to develop tolerance within a short time, just as they do with Alcohol and Heroin, and to fail to induce pleasure and serenity.

Research activities intended to develop an ideal anti-depressant continue. For example, there is now a growing recognition that there exists a "happiness gene" that operates in those fortunate, enviable people who always seem to be cheerful! Genetic studies have proved that happiness and psychological stability are linked to the existence of two copies (one from both parents) of a gene called 5-HTTLPR, which was found to be responsible for the transport of Serotonin in the brain. Possibly, there could be more "happiness" genes.

All that remains for us to do is to hope that Pharmacology, or the developing science of Gene Therapy will allow us, still in our life-time, to reach the state of mind that was advocated by Guru Meher Baba: "Don't worry, be happy!"

Printed in the United States
by Baker & Taylor Publisher Services